THE
MUTANT
MUSHROOM
TAKEOVER

Also by Summer Rachel Short

Attack of the Killer Komodos: A Maggie and Nate Mystery

THE MUTANT MUSHROOM TAKEOVER

A MAGGIE AND NATE MYSTERY

Summer Rachel Short

Simon & Schuster Books for Young Readers

NEW YORK   LONDON   TORONTO   SYDNEY   NEW DELHI

SIMON & SCHUSTER BOOKS FOR YOUNG READERS
An imprint of Simon & Schuster Children's Publishing Division
1230 Avenue of the Americas, New York, New York 10020
This book is a work of fiction. Any references to historical events, real people, or real places are used fictitiously. Other names, characters, places, and events are products of the author's imagination, and any resemblance to actual events or places or persons, living or dead, is entirely coincidental.
Text © 2020 by Summer Rachel Short
Cover illustrations © 2020 by DKNG Studios
Cover design by Lizzy Bromley © 2020 by Simon & Schuster, Inc.
All rights reserved, including the right of reproduction in whole or in part in any form.
SIMON & SCHUSTER BOOKS FOR YOUNG READERS
and related marks are trademarks of Simon & Schuster, Inc.
For information about special discounts for bulk purchases, please contact
Simon & Schuster Special Sales at 1-866-506-1949 or business@simonandschuster.com.
The Simon & Schuster Speakers Bureau can bring authors to your live event.
For more information or to book an event, contact the Simon & Schuster Speakers Bureau at
1-866-248-3049 or visit our website at www.simonspeakers.com.
Also available in a Simon & Schuster Books for Young Readers hardcover edition
Interior design by Hilary Zarycky
The text for this book was set in Adobe Caslon Pro.
Manufactured in the United States of America
0821 OFF
First Simon & Schuster Books for Young Readers paperback edition September 2021
2 4 6 8 10 9 7 5 3 1
The Library of Congress has cataloged the hardcover edition as follows:
Names: Short, Summer Rachel, author.
Title: The mutant mushroom takeover / Summer Rachel Short.
Description: First edition. | New York : Simon & Schuster Books for Young Readers, [2020] |
Audience: Ages 8–12. | Audience: Grades 4–6. | Summary: Hoping to restore her father's
good name and job, Maggie teams up with friend Nate to win a junior naturalist contest, but the
rare bioluminescent fungus they find is big trouble. Includes facts about fungi.
Identifiers: LCCN 2019048730 (print) | LCCN 2019048731 (eBook) | ISBN 9781534468658
(hardcover) | ISBN 9781534468665 (pbk) | ISBN 9781534468672 (eBook)
Subjects: CYAC: Mushrooms—Fiction. | Bioluminescence—Fiction. | Best friends—Fiction. |
Friendship—Fiction. | Fathers and daughters—Fiction. | Science fiction.
Classification: LCC PZ7.1.S51782 Mut 2020 (print) | LCC PZ7.1.S51782 (eBook) |
DDC [Fic]—dc23
LC record available at https://lccn.loc.gov/2019048730
LC eBook record available at https://lccn.loc.gov/2019048731

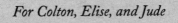

For Colton, Elise, and Jude

CHAPTER ONE

This is one marvelous mutant. A bona fide scientific wonder.

The black and gold moth flutters to the over-grown honeysuckle bush. It's the *Hemaris diffinis*, more commonly known as the bumblebee moth. But this is no ordinary specimen. This baby's got a third antenna sprouting from the tip-top of its head—tall and skinny with a dusty bulb at the end.

I creep forward and focus the camera's lens—it's vintage 1998 and requires a little finessing. I'm milliseconds from snapping the picture of a lifetime when a door behind me bangs open. An orange sneaker zips past my nose toward the moth. The *Hemaris diffinis* dodges it, sailing high above my mobile home's aluminum roof and well out of photographic range.

I whirl around. "Nate Fulton! Are you trying to ruin my life?"

"What?" Nate frowns, his face so red in the blazing

Texas heat that his freckles nearly go camo. "I probably just saved your life, Mags. Remember what happened to my Uncle Tony last summer? Nearly died when that swarm of bees went up his swim trunks. Stung his butt, like, a hundred times. Got anna-flap-tick shock."

"It's anaphylactic, and that wasn't a bee. It was an ultra-rare mutant moth. I needed that photo!"

"For the contest thing?" Nate retrieves the sneaker and stuffs his toes back inside.

"It's more than a contest. It's Vitaccino's Junior Naturalist Merit Award. There's five hundred big ones at stake, plus a meeting with the head honchos. For the winners, anyway." I scan the sky. The moth is nowhere to be seen. I slump to the ground and lean my back against the side of the trailer. Without the *Hemaris diffinis*, there's no Merit Award and zero chance to make my case in front of the board of directors. My one shot for smoothing things over for Dad and bringing him back home to Shady Pines.

Nate straightens his Darth Vader ball cap. "I didn't know it was a mutant moth. I'm no bugologist or anything."

"Entomologist." I rip a honeysuckle from the vine.

Nate rocks forward on his toes. "I know something that'll cheer you up."

I sip the honeysuckle's syrupy nectar. "What if I don't want to cheer up?"

"Come on, Maggie. I've got news. I'm talking top-secret intel."

I sigh. Nate's intel could be anything from finding half a pack of gum in his shorts to buying a rare issue of *Midnight Kingdom* at the comic book store. "Spill it."

Nate looks over his shoulder and drops his voice. "Not here."

I follow his gaze. Glory, Nate's hefty basset hound, is passed out in the weedy grass in front of his place. Otherwise, the trailer park is deserted.

"Headquarters." He nods to the tree house between our trailers. The roof is rusty siding and the walls are discarded plywood. All of it's held together with a combination of duct tape, nails, and bungee cords. It doesn't look like much on the outside, but behind those walls are treasures like binoculars, fun-size bags of chips, and loads of old *Nat Geo* magazines. Our own private paradise.

Normally I'd shoot up that ladder like nobody's business, but Shady Pines summers are brutal. Sweat's already dripping down my back from chasing the bumblebee moth and I'm not sure I feel like hauling up the rope ladder for a bit of alleged news. "Pass." I tug my knees to my chest. This wasn't my first try for a prize-worthy photo, but those got botched too. Turns out opening the film canister to check on things is a big no-no with these old-timey cameras. That moth was my last hope.

Nate raises one hand, shielding his eyes. "Her death-ray glare . . . saps the life from my . . . bones." He stumbles forward with a moan like he's dying a slow, torturous death.

When I don't say anything, he cracks one eye open. "I'm dying here, Mags. You really want that on your conscience?"

I should probably stay mad to teach Nate to quit butting in where he doesn't belong, but I know he's got a bottomless repertoire of dramatic noises he'll unleash until I give in. "Fine. You're forgiven."

I thrust out one arm.

Nate grabs my hand and pulls me up. "You're a lifesaver, Mags."

"Uh-huh." I trudge up the tree house ladder. "This better be worth it."

"Oh, it is," he promises as we slide onto the well-worn wooden slats at the top. Up here, we can see half the town—from Marble Falls, the fancy-pants neighborhood with the bad luck to share a border with Raccoon Creek Trailer Park, to the humongous green forest beyond.

I squish down into a red beanbag chair. "So, what's the big scoop?"

"You're gonna love it." Nate grins. "My cousin Ricky came over this afternoon while I was nuking some corn dogs. He said he and his buddies were passing by Old

Man Bell's woods last night. Minding their own business, more or less. They saw something, Maggie. I'm talking confirmed paranormal phenomenon." His eyes go all wide and mysterious, like the time he was sure aliens were making crop circles in Jerry Able's cornfields. "Ghost lights."

I stretch out my legs and cross my ankles. Ricky's fourteen, and all he talks about are girls and racing his beat-up dirt bike. "It's probably just security lights. All the houses in Marble Falls are getting them."

"Ricky said the forest was glowing green and blue. The guys didn't get too close, but Ricky was pretty sure the trees were moaning his name. This thing has *The Conspiracy Squad* written all over it."

I should've known this had something to do with Nate's YouTube channel. Every couple of weeks he puts out a new video and I usually get roped into it somehow or other. Last month it was snooping around the Thurston County Animal Shelter on the hunt for werewolves. It was a bust. But we did get to snuggle some super adorable calico kittens. Nate's convinced *The Conspiracy Squad* is gonna go viral someday soon and rake in the big bucks. And maybe it will. But right now he's only got about five subscribers, plus a few wack jobs who leave comments about Martians communicating with them through the fillings in their teeth.

Nate seems to read the hesitation on my face and starts

up again. "You can't pass up an opportunity like this. It's once-in-a-lifetime good. Old Man Bell's woods are already creepy and probably haunted by, like, a bajillion ghosts."

"How's that a selling point?"

"Uh, 'cause it sounds totally awesome. And now that we've got solid reports of paranormal happenings, we'd be nuts not to check it out."

I don't believe in ghosts, but the place does stir something cold and creaky in the pit of my stomach. Around town there are a thousand different rumors about the old man and his land. Some say the place is cursed and that strange people walk the woods at night. Others say he catches kids and cooks them up in his oven, like the witch from *Hansel and Gretel*. Either way, I've always steered clear.

Nate cracks his knuckles. "What do you say, Mags? You in?"

"Those woods have NO TRESPASSING signs all around them. I can't risk getting busted. They don't give Merit Awards to eleven-year-old criminals. Besides, I've gotta finish my application." Though without the pictures of the bumblebee moth, I'll need to come up with something else quick. The application has to be postmarked by tomorrow.

"You wanna study bugs and trees, right? What better

place to go than Old Man Bell's ginormous woods? I'm practically handing you your Junior Science Nerd badge on a platter."

"There's no badge. It's a cash prize and a meeting with the board, remember?"

"Whatever." He spins his hat around backward. "Are you going to investigate with me or not?"

I strum my fingers on the wooden floor. Nate has a point. Old Man Bell's woods offer hundreds of acres of unexplored wildlife. "We'd have to be in and out. Snap a few photos and then scram."

"Totally. In and out. No sweat."

It's risky, but I need that award. "Well, what's the plan?"

Nate steeples his fingers like an evil genius plotting his Greater Thurston County takeover. "Assemble our gear and meet outside Headquarters after sundown. We've got to be ready for anything. Ghosts, vampires, aliens."

"Or security lights. Don't forget about that possibility."

Nate reaches for the rope ladder. "Rendezvous at twenty-one-hundred hours."

"Is that nine or ten o'clock?"

"Check the Zombie Apocalypse Survivor Guide I gave you last Christmas."

"Couldn't you just tell me?"

Nate's already halfway down the ladder. "And don't forget the garlic!"

I hang my head over the edge of the tree house. "Garlic?"

"In case of glowing vampires. Sheesh Mags, stay with me."

Nate drops to the ground and trots off to his trailer. As I head down the ladder, there's a hum in the distance. Right on schedule, a crop duster flies low over Old Man Bell's land. White rains down from the little plane. I've always wondered why a place that doesn't produce any crops needs a daily dose of herbicides or whatever's in that thing. But who knows what Old Man Bell's thinking? He's an eccentric hermit. Maybe he just really hates weeds.

CHAPTER TWO

I open the fridge and peek in at an assortment of leftover casseroles. Ever since my older brother, Ezra, and I moved in with Gramma six months ago, I've eaten about a thousand pounds of tuna noodle skradoodle and kitchen sink cowboy stew.

I lift the foil on a pie pan, only to discover Ezra's polished off the last of the lemon meringue and left the empty plate in the fridge. *Greedy guts.* I put the pan in the sink and grab a tub of cheesy shells with sliced hotdog weenies. While the bowl spins in the microwave, I scan the spice rack. Gramma's got three different types of garlicky powders. I toss a half-empty bottle of garlic salt in my backpack. That'll have to do for warding off Nate's glow-in-the-dark vampires.

There's still a few hours till we kick off Operation Get Arrested for Trespassing on Creepy Old Dude's Property. I eye the desktop computer in the breakfast nook. It's been three days since I last talked to Dad. That's close to a record for us. He's been working at a remote site this week and hasn't had cell or e-mail coverage. I munch a mouthful of cheesy shells. It's not like it'll hurt to send him another message. He can just read them all at once when he gets back to civilization. I slide into the swivel chair, open my e-mail, and start typing.

To: tommy.stone@nps.gov
From: maggieheartsnature@gmail.com
Subject: Hemaris diffinis
Hi Dad,
I almost got a photo of a rare moth today. It looked just like a huge bumblebee and reminded me of the ones buzzing around the bluebonnets on our trip to Fredericksburg.

Anyway, I saw a For Sale sign on a little house down the street from our old place. I know you said I should let you handle that kind of stuff, but this is too good of an opportunity to pass up. Just think, if we bought it, things could go back to the way they were before. This new place won't have Long-Legged Louisa or the Explorer room, but that's okay. We could plant another willow tree and wallpaper a new room with maps and pictures of volcanoes and rivers.

Also, I think Gramma's trailer might be shrinking.

Probably because Ezra has been eating so much pie.
He's taller than Gramma now. I'm getting tall too.
    Just say the word and I'll call the realtor. I bet
she'd give me a free tour.
Love you to the moon and back,
Maggie

Six months ago, Dad got fired from his lab assistant
job at Vitaccino headquarters. I don't know all the details,
but somehow a bunch of rats ended up swimming around
in a vat of the company's health drink. It turned out to
be terrible timing. The health department showed up that
morning and shut the whole place down for a week.

Dad looked around for other work but didn't have
much luck. He said science jobs were hard to come by
in a small town. A month later, we were packing up our
perfect blue house on Maple Street. Dad got hired as a
park ranger in Yellowstone, and Ezra and I moved in with
Gramma. But this is all temporary.

Dad's old company is big into giving back to the community. The owners, Charles and Lydia Croft, are always
doing nice stuff like sponsoring school pizza parties or
giving smart kids college scholarships. And now they're
offering the Junior Naturalist Merit Award, plus a face-
to-face meeting with their board of directors. When I
score that award and get in front of the powers that be,

I'll be on my way to getting Dad his job back and moving him home where he belongs.

I jiggle the mouse, ready to hit send.

"Tell your daddy I mailed him a package of those turtle brownies he likes. But he better eat this batch quicker or the critters will steal it, too," a voice over my shoulder advises.

I frown. "You shouldn't read other people's mail, Gramma."

"I only skimmed it." Gramma shrugs. She's already in her white cook's uniform for her shift at Sunny Day Nursing Home. One wrist is loaded with jingling bangles and her short silvery hair is puffed up with too much hairspray. Streaks of bright pink blush stand out against her otherwise pale and slightly wrinkly skin. "And let him know I saw a NOW HIRING sign at Lenny's Supermarket. I could put in a good word for him, you know."

"He's a biologist, Gramma. He doesn't want to work as a check-out boy."

"Well, beggars can't be choosers. That's what I always say."

I don't bother arguing with Gramma. We both want Dad home, but we've got different ideas on how to go about it.

Gramma pulls her purse strap over her shoulder and heads for the door. "I'll be back by ten. There's a pot of beef and barley stew in the fridge and a fresh batch of molasses cookies in the jar. Make sure you turn off the burner when you're done warming things up."

"Yes, ma'am." But there won't be time for beef and barley tonight. Not with the Merit Award at stake. I grab my backpack and head to my room for the rest of the supplies.

Lennox, my leopard gecko, scurries in his terrarium, as my orange tabby, Pascal, flicks his tail and gazes devilishly at the black and white spotted lizard. "Don't get any ideas. Lennox is family." Pascal stares back at me with unconvinced golden eyes.

I rummage under my bed to find my old Dora the Explorer flashlight. It's too babyish for an up-and-coming naturalist, but it's Dora or we walk in the dark. I reach for my camera—really, it's Dad's. It's got a telescoping lens, detachable flash, and takes 35mm film. I found it on the top shelf of the hall closet a couple of months ago. Gramma said it was finders keepers, and that Dad could reclaim it when he came on home.

The light in my room gradually shifts to a dingy yellow. I lift the blinds. The trees are dark silhouettes against a gray sky. A streaky cloud drifts across the horizon. If I squint, it looks like a face with a gaping mouth and too-sharp teeth. My stomach does a mini-loop, and I pull the jar of garlic salt out of my bag. I sprinkle a good-size pinch on my tank top and shorts, then head for the door. I'm not being superstitious, just prepared. Vampires aren't real, but vampire bats are. And they carry rabies.

CHAPTER THREE

The sky is murky purple when I lock the trailer's door. I jog to Headquarters, where Nate waits under the old oak tree.

He sniffs. "We'll definitely be safe from vampires tonight."

"I may have over-sprinkled." I shake the collar of my shirt and garlic salt drifts to the ground.

We pass a few trailers on the gravel road out of Raccoon Creek and then turn onto the path that winds toward the gated entrance of Marble Falls. That's when I spot trouble.

My brother coasts down the middle of the road on his skateboard. Like me, Ezra's kinda skinny with lanky brown hair. Only he's pastier from spending too much time holed up in his room staring at his phone. Tonight he's wearing his usual black T-shirt, black skinny jeans, and black high-top sneakers. I don't know if it's some kind of fashion statement or if he just hates color since turning thirteen. His friends Jack and Zion skateboard nearby.

"Hey, Ezra." Nate waves with way too much enthusiasm. "What's happening, my man?"

"Not a lot." Ezra ollies two feet into the air, lands it, then glides our way.

I pull Nate's arm. If Ezra finds out we're going to check out an alleged ghost light, he'll never let me live it down. "Come on. We've got places to be."

"Oh yeah, and where's that?" Ezra pops his skateboard into one hand. The back wheels cling on with a thick band of duct tape.

"None of your—"

"We're investigating the greatest mystery Thurston County has ever known," Nate blurts.

I jab him in the side. He's always falling for Ezra's cool-older-brother vibe.

"Impressive," Ezra says in a tone that's anything but impressed.

"Yup." Nate bobs his head. "Confirmed paranormal activity. We'll probably be on the news tonight. Stay tuned."

My cheeks heat up. Ezra's barely stopped teasing me about sneaking into the Marble Falls cabanas last spring in search of what Nate had deemed "irrefutable proof of Bigfoot."

Jack and Zion quit skating and come to Ezra's side. Jack swings his skateboard into one hand. Jack's like a taller, bulkier version of Ezra. All black clothes, slouchy shoulders, and a perpetual look of boredom. "So what mystery are you two gonna solve today? Somebody pee in the Shady Pines city pool?"

"It's nothing," I say. "Just some lights."

"It's not just any ol' lights," Nate cuts in. "We have it on good authority that some crazy ghost lights are flashing down at Old Man Bell's place."

I stomp his foot with my heel. "It's really more of a scientific exploration than anything."

"Ghost lights?" Ezra grins at Jack and Zion.

"Yep." Nate gives his foot a shake and then strolls ahead with a little extra pep in his step.

"I heard those woods were haunted," Zion says, flipping dark curls off his forehead. Zion's slim with brown skin and light eyes, and unlike the other two, still manages to smile every once in a while.

"Could be," Nate offers. "I wouldn't be surprised if those lights were the ghosts of dead Bells from, like, the last hundred years. But till I get a closer look I can't rule out UFOs or vampires."

Ezra drops his board to the ground. "We're totally checking it out."

Jack shrugs. "Better than standing around here."

Wheels hit the pavement.

"Thanks for the heads up, little dude," Ezra calls as the three of them zip past us.

"Wait!" Nate yells, chasing after them until they take a curve in the road and disappear. When I catch up to Nate, he shakes his head looking dumbstruck. "That was our investigation."

"And they're totally stealing it." A mosquito whines near my ear, and I slap my cheek as we pass the NOW LEAVING SHADY PINES sign.

Nate kicks a pebble. "I just thought it might be sorta fun if we all went together. Like our own team of Ghostbusters."

The first few stars peek out above and the smell of summer hay wafts from the fields on either side of us. If I'm honest, I wouldn't have minded playing Ghostbusters with Ezra for a couple of hours. But unlike Nate, I know that's not gonna happen. Ever since Dad left, my brother's pretty much allergic to fun. "Probably wasn't much to see anyway."

We drift down the dirt road past the knee-high golden crops that buzz with cicadas. The night air feels sticky and too thick.

"You know, we could still catch up." Nate nods toward the curve in the road where the guys disappeared. "If you don't mind getting a bit dirty."

I give him a sideways smile. "No self-respecting naturalist is afraid of a little dirt."

He grins and we take off at full speed, leaping over the

railroad tracks and scuttling down a narrow path partially hidden by tangles of dewberry brambles. When we finally make it to the woods, we're panting hard. The guys' skateboards are propped against a cypress tree with swaths of moss dangling from its branches like shaggy beards. Under the thick canopy, it's too dark to see much. I've got no choice but to bust out the Dora flashlight.

NO TRESPASSING signs hang from every tree. I grip the camera's strap, a fresh wave of doubt rising in my stomach. If we keep going, we're lawbreakers.

Nate studies my face. "It's just this once, Mags, and it's for a good cause. Scientific research."

All my plans for Dad hinge on winning the Merit Award and getting in front of the Vitaccino board of directors. If I back down now, I can kiss those dreams goodbye. "Ten minutes."

"Perfecto. That's all I need for a bit of B-roll." Nate dances ahead, shaking his backside and shimmying his shoulders.

I bite back a smile. Nate's one of those people who can pull off being quirky without seeming bonkers. Like the time he showed up at school in a homemade Loki costume. It wasn't Halloween or anything. Even grumpy old Ms. Odgin got a kick out of it.

As Nate and I weave through the trees, something flickers in the distance like a handful of glitter flung into the air. I stop walking. All around us, the tree trunks begin to tremble with light. Neon blue, nuclear green. The wind howls and the hair on the back of my neck stands on end.

"What is all this stuff?" Nate asks. The glimmer reflects off his eyes and makes them twinkle aquamarine.

I stretch out my hand to touch a luminous green patch carpeting the bone-white bark of a sycamore tree. "Definitely not security lights."

CHAPTER FOUR

For a moment, I forget to breathe. A glowing indigo jelly trickles down a dead log like electric blueberry jam. I spin around. Fleshy neon stars pulse along the tree trunks. It's a wonderland of color and lights. This must be how Madam Curie felt when she discovered radium.

"This is so going viral." Nate holds his camcorder out, filming the woods. "We are standing in what is likely the site of the latest UFO landing," he says in a slow, dramatic voice. "Solid proof that extraterrestrials are among us."

I suddenly remember what I'm here for—and it isn't an alien investigation. I lift Dad's camera off my neck and kneel next to a tree with radiant teal lace swirling around its roots. I adjust the camera's focus and snap a picture. This is even better than the bumblebee moth with the bonus antenna. The Merit Award is mine.

Nate zigzags around the trees and then bounces to my side. "So, what's your take? UFO? Shapeshifters? Vampires?"

I brush a twig against a patch of blue that shimmers like a sea of sapphires. I smile. "You were right, Nate. These woods are amazing, but it isn't anything supernatural. It's bioluminescence."

Nate's eyes narrow. "Please tell me you're not turning the most awesome night of my life into something boring and sciencey."

"Bioluminescence is a scientific wonder. Some things in nature can produce their own light—fireflies, jellyfish, and . . ." I pause, taking a closer look at the fleshy stuff at the bottom of the tree. "Certain kinds of fungi."

"Fungi? As in mushrooms?"

"And things like mold and yeast."

"You are literally killing me right now." Nate pitches his head back. "What about evil mushrooms? There's still hope for that, right?"

I poke a few swirly emerald bulbs with a dried leaf, trying to remember a *Nat Geo* article I read a couple of years ago. "Most bioluminescent species grow where it's dark and wet. The canopy here blocks the sun, and we get plenty of rain." I scan the fluorescent trails spiraling up all around us and sigh. "Nature's really incredible."

Nate groans. "'Nature's really incredible,' won't propel me to Internet stardom, Maggie. You gotta give me something spicy. I need the unexplained. The weird. The terrifying."

"A lot of mushrooms are poisonous and can give you terrible diarrhea. That's pretty scary."

"Fantastic. They can write, 'Watch out for diarrhea,' as my yearbook quote. That's not the kinda legacy I'm looking to make." Nate pushes both hands through his hair, fluffing his curls into wild heaps. His eyes suddenly bulge and he jumps back. "SPIDER!" A quarter-size wolf spider crawls up his bare leg. "Get it, Mags! Before it makes webs in my ears!"

"Calm down—wolf spiders don't even make webs!"

"I feel its fangs piercing my flesh!"

I roll my eyes and try to get ahold of Nate's leg, but he's gyrating so much it's impossible.

Nate flings his body out in a dramatic ninja kick, and the spider finally loses its grip. He whimpers and falls back, his feet bashing against a log. A teal cloud explodes out of the dead wood, making tiny fireworks around Nate's sneaker. He scuttles back. "What was that? Say it's not more spiders. Or spider eggs. Or anything related to spiders."

I kneel and examine the log. "I think the cloud was . . . spores. That's how fungi reproduce, like flowers with pollen."

He jumps to his feet. "Do spores sometimes hatch into baby spiders?"

"You really need to do your homework sometime," I say and snap a few more photos of the woods.

Voices stir behind us. I grab the flashlight and spin

around. It's Ezra, Zion, and Jack, laughing and jumping through the woods like it's their own personal playground.

Then something makes a whizzing sound and a stream of white sprays out from a can in Ezra's hand. He's coating a tree with the outline of a ghost. "Ezra, stop!"

Instead of stopping, he turns and sprays another tree. "I'm just giving the place a little more style."

"Don't!" I yell. Ezra got suspended last spring for tagging the boys' bathroom. Gramma nearly blew a blood vessel. And Dad spent his entire Easter visit paying extra attention to Ezra. Like if they bonded enough over the weekend it'd make Ezra nice again. "You don't have to mark your territory everywhere you go. You're not a dog."

He raises his chin to the sky and howls, then finishes the second ghost and tosses the spray can on the ground.

I scoop up his litter. "Did you even stop to look around before you started destroying things? This is a one-of-a-kind biosphere and all you want to do is mess it up."

"You know what this stuff is?" Ezra asks. Jack and Zion shuffle a little closer, looking slightly less bored than usual.

I toss the spray can into my backpack. "It's bioluminescent fungi. The light's caused by a chemical reaction inside the mushrooms."

"You don't have to show off, Maggie. Dad's not here to be impressed by all your dumb nature stuff."

Ezra's always got something snarky to say about Dad

lately. It's like he's forgotten that six months ago Dad was his favorite person on the planet.

Ezra looks me over then blows out a puff of air. "Look, I was just joking, all right?" He rubs his knuckles over the top of my head, and my thoughts jump back to the three of us loaded into Dad's pickup. Eating sunflower seeds and drinking bottles of root beer. Crossing miles of highway while Dad told us about Greenland sharks that can live for five hundred years in icy arctic waters, or Appalachian millipedes that spray cyanide poison to scare off predators. Ezra would give him a big fake yawn and act like he was bored, but then he'd lean back and keep right on listening. He loved Dad's stories as much as I did. Only now he doesn't remember any of that.

I push Ezra's hand away. "Dad's going to be back soon. And he's not going to like it if you get yourself into more trouble."

"You know, not everybody who leaves comes home again, Mags."

I swallow. Ezra isn't talking about Dad anymore. I don't remember much about her. Only long, silky hair and snippets of "Twinkle, Twinkle, Little Star." Ezra remembers, though. He used to tell me stories about the way things were when Mom was still around. But nowadays he won't talk to me about anything. "Dad's not like that," I say. "You'll see."

"Sure, whatever." Ezra yanks on the straps of his backpack. "I'm outta here. There's no ghosts. Just a bunch of mushroom junk."

As he turns to go, a beastly growl rumbles in the distance. Moonlight catches the dark forms of three large doberman pinschers.

Jack scrambles back. "Nobody said anything about watchdogs."

"This wasn't exactly an official tour," Nate replies.

Their snarls grow fiercer as they stalk closer. My heart thumps in my ears. We're trespassing and these dogs are going to make us pay.

CHAPTER FIVE

The dobermans charge toward us, racing over gnarled roots and ropey vines. The dogs are solid muscle with eyes that glisten green in the darkness. Zion and Jack start sprinting away. I'm close behind, but when my shoelaces catch under my foot, I crash to the dirt.

Nate skids to a stop. "They're coming, Mags! Get up!"

The dogs fly toward us. I squeeze my eyes shut. We're going to get eaten alive. Gramma will find my shredded body and wear black for the rest of her life and tell everyone that back in her day kids didn't trespass or get mauled by dogs.

"Come here, boy. Nice boy. Easy." I peek up. Ezra's wagging a big stick and patting one leg. The dobermans turn and circle him. Their lips curl, showing sharp white fangs. One of the dogs springs forward and sinks its teeth into the bottom of Ezra's jeans. The fabric rips, and Ezra stumbles back. The dogs stalk closer, and Ezra covers his face with his hands. The closest dog opens its mouth, ready to tear him to bits. But the wind suddenly picks up, rushing through the trees as loud as a freight train.

Nate slaps both hands over his ears. "What the heck is that?"

There's a low moan that at first I think is one of the dogs. Only it sounds too human. The dobermans whimper, then duck their heads and run.

Ezra sits up, looking pale and shocked to still be in one piece. "What just happened?"

I reach for my flashlight and shine it down a winding path. The dogs are nowhere to be seen. Leaves rustle and yellow light flickers as something tall and dark swishes through the woods. Another moan splits the silence. Those dogs may not be the worst thing we meet tonight.

The air's charged, like the feeling just before a thunderclap. A figure steps into view. His long white beard sways in the wind and the light from his lantern casts shadows over his leathery face. But it's no ghost. It's Hiram Bell, the creaky old hermit himself. Crumpled hat, dusty overalls, and muddy boots. He looks exactly how I imagine Rip Van Winkle would after his twenty-year sleep.

Nate hops to his feet. "We gotta bail, Mags."

"Hold your horses, whippersnappers." Old Man Bell shuffles toward us, all three dogs at his side. "I'm hauling you in to the authorities."

"We wanted to see the lights, sir." I stand and dust bits of twigs and leaves off my shorts. "We didn't mean any harm."

"Didn't mean no harm? Tromping through the place, smashing things up. That's what I call vandalism." He doesn't mention the actual vandalism—Ezra's tree graffiti. Most likely he hasn't spotted it yet, but I'm betting that if he does, he'll sic the dobermans on us and we'll all be dog jerky for sure.

Bell gives a long, drawn-out cough like an old truck struggling to start up. "These woods ain't the place to stand around jabbering. You mischief-makers follow me. We're settling this tonight."

The lights in the forest quiver and Bell's head rears up. The wind whooshes like somebody just turned on an industrial-strength hair dryer. The dogs tuck themselves between Bell's legs as misty white fog whirls up from the ground. Old Man Bell shakes his fist in the air. "This ain't the time for your nonsense! Go on, get outta here!"

"Is he talking to us?" I whisper. I still don't believe in ghosts but I do believe in unstable psychopaths.

"The dude's spent way too much time alone," Nate murmurs.

"We're getting out of here. Now." Ezra grabs the collar of my shirt and tugs.

The fog fans out like a giant squeeze of baby powder. All at once, the glowing fungi go dark.

"You better quit that or you'll be sorry!" Bell scuttles

away from the cloud at an impressive speed for such an old guy.

"There's no one else here," I call, afraid Old Man Bell might really be losing it.

His eyes lock on the swirling mist. Everything goes still. In a flash, the fog puffs up and envelopes Bell in murky white. I hold my breath and shine my flashlight, searching for some sign that he's still there.

When the cloud thins, Bell's doubled over with both hands on his knees. He's wheezing hard and his face lights up with a pea soup green glow. The dogs circle him, their fur bristling around their collars. A hacking cough rakes through Bell again. He sways side to side then crumples to the ground.

"We need to do something," I yell. This night is a disaster. We never should've come to these woods.

"Like what?" Nate asks. "Please don't say mouth-to-mouth resuscitation."

Ezra's so quiet that I glance back, wondering if he's already bolted. Instead, his hands are bunched up at his sides, like he's psyching himself up for the world's biggest ollie. For an instant it's like the old days when I could look at him and know what he was thinking without him saying a word. And right now, I know Ezra's not going to run.

"You and Nate get out of here. I'll meet you on the road in a minute," Ezra says, then jogs toward Bell.

"What's he doing?" Nate asks.

My heart's hammering like crazy but a small piece of it can't help but feel proud. "He's going to help." When we were little, Ezra told everybody he'd be a doctor one day. He carried around a bag with bandages and Life Savers he pretended were medicine. Seeing somebody hurt or sick always twisted him up. But I'd figured that part of him was gone.

Ezra kneels by Old Man Bell's side. "These woods ain't safe for you," Bell wheezes.

Ezra pulls his phone from his pocket. "I'm calling for help."

Bell groans, and the dogs come closer, nudging Bell with their noses. "Don't bring nobody else here." Sparkling blue dots prick along his arms like thousands of lightning bugs signaling in the night. I want to run, but I can't take my eyes off of him. "Don't let it out. Promise me, boy."

"Sure, okay," Ezra stammers, then talks into the phone. "We need help at Old Man Bell's place. Something's really wrong with him."

"It's too late. You—" Bell's words break off into another fit of coughing. When he finally quits, he pulls Ezra close and murmurs something in his ear. Ezra peers down at Bell with a mixed-up expression. With another racking cough, glowing teal embers fly from Bell's mouth onto Ezra's face. Ezra winces and wipes one hand across his cheeks, but he only manages to smear the shining dust over his skin, giving him a swampy green hue. My stomach twists and I get the same sick feeling I had when Ezra fell off a ladder a couple of years ago. Only this time, I don't think hydrogen peroxide or an Ace bandage are the answer.

Nate cringes. "This is the part in the movies where the monsters come out and everybody dies."

Bell's coughing finally calms down, and the old man goes limp. The howling wind and the swirling fog have vanished. The forest goes still like the hard silence that comes after a big argument. Then Bell's dogs arch their necks and howl. It's a sad, lonesome sound. A shiver zings down my back.

CHAPTER SIX

The forest lights up again, blazing brighter than
ever. A white whirlwind spins around Bell and
Ezra, stirring my brother's hair into powdery
tangles.

"It's back!" Nate ducks his head.

As the wind howls, I tell myself that monsters aren't
real. We're not gonna be sucked up into the cloud and
vaporized. My heart will not explode with terror. That's
scientifically impossible. I think.

Then, like a door slammed shut, the swirling funnel is
gone.

"We gotta go." Ezra hops to his feet and gives Bell a
final look. The old man lies motionless under the wide oak
tree, his dogs hovering at his sides. The three of us dash
through the tall grass that borders the woods. My legs feel
slow and heavy, as if dozens of dumbbells are tied to my
sneakers.

Near the railroad tracks, Jack and Zion pace back and

forth. When they spot us, they jog to Ezra. "Did Old Man Bell call the sheriff? Are we busted?" Jack asks, his fingers twitching at the top of his skateboard.

Ezra doesn't answer and instead keeps marching past him.

There's a droning siren, and then the flashing red and blue lights as the sheriff's truck bumps along the dirt road. When it skids to a stop, Sheriff Huxley and Deputy Ronald leap out, both wearing cowboy hats as big as the truck's wheels.

The sheriff grabs a first-aid kit from the pickup bed, and the deputy tucks a stretcher under his arm. "You kids did the right thing calling this in," the sheriff says, dipping his head our way. "We'll take it from here."

As the pair hustle through the forest scrub, Ezra grabs his skateboard and reaches for my arm. Sparks of aquamarine flicker from his hands. "It's time to go, Mags. There's nothing else to see here."

I wriggle my arm free. "I'll be there in a sec."

Ezra grunts and starts walking. Jack and Zion trot along after him, leaving me and Nate alone in the moonlit clearing.

I glance back at the woods, searching for traces of the electric colors we just discovered. But everything's gone dark now.

"That didn't turn out like I was hoping," Nate says.

As we trudge home, I want to say something encouraging, but I can't find the words. I can't explain what we just saw. I know old people can get sick. Have sudden heart attacks or strokes. But this was different. And somehow, talking about any of it feels like it will make it more real. So I stuff down my questions and keep walking along the dusty country road.

"Did you hear what Bell said about the woods?" Nate asks, stirring up a little puff of dirt with each step.

My stomach twists. "That they weren't safe."

"Then that blue cloud came out of him. It looked like the glowing stuff from the mushrooms. You think that might've been what made him sick?"

My best guess is that the glowing dust was spores. But if that's what came out of Old Man Bell, something was seriously off. People shouldn't just fill up with spores. "I don't know."

Nate nods and scrunches his face like he's mulling over a question. "He was pretty close to your brother when all that went down."

"Yeah. I saw that too." I wish I could laugh it all off. But this time we're not dealing with a crop circle conspiracy or would-be werewolves.

"Maybe mushrooms are freakier than I thought." Nate stuffs his hands in his pockets and doesn't say anything else.

When we turn in to Raccoon Creek, Gramma's car is parked in front of our trailer. June bugs circle the flickering porch lights and tree frogs chirp in the distance.

"You gonna tell your gramma what happened?" Nate asks.

I shake my head. "Nope. You gonna tell your parents?"

"Nah. They already think *The Conspiracy Squad* is a bad influence."

I wave good night, hoping Gramma won't question me. She has a sixth sense for sniffing out what she calls "funny business."

The TV flashes a rainbow of light over the dim living room. Gramma's slumped in her recliner, snoring softly. I tiptoe past her, heading for my room. There's a loud cough, and I spin around.

Ezra's stretched out on the couch. "Hey, Mags." He sits up and blinks innocently like he's been loafing around the house all night.

I eye Gramma. "She say anything when you came in?"

"She's out cold." For an instant, Ezra's lips look blue—like he's been sucking on cotton candy–flavored Popsicles. Then the image on the TV changes and the color fades away.

I fiddle with the camera's strap. Part of me wants to talk things over with Ezra. To figure out what just happened and untangle all the knots in the pit of my stomach.

But before I can put any of my feelings into a question, a muffled grunt comes from Gramma's chair.

Her eyes flutter open. "You just now coming in?"

"Yes, ma'am." I try to sound casual but can't quite meet her eye.

"It's awful late, Magnolia. What were you doing?"

"Hanging out with Nate."

"I suppose I could've guessed that." She pats her hair. It's a mix of flattened-down silver locks and wild fluffy tufts. "Did you eat yet? I can warm you up a plate." Gramma starts to stand, but she's not quite awake yet and wobbles back into the chair.

"I'm not hungry." My tongue feels like a tangled-up Slinky. All of a sudden, I don't want to keep this inside. As I open my mouth to spill everything, Ezra shakes his head and mouths, "No." There's a panicked look in his eyes that dries up my big confession.

I've kept secrets from Gramma before, but this is different. Trespassing, the whirling white cloud, Bell's glowing skin. That's a lot of stuff to keep in. "I'm gonna take a shower. Night, Gramma."

"G'night. Don't forget to scrub behind your ears and in between your toes."

It's the same reminder Gramma gives me every night. Normally I have to fight the urge to roll my eyes, but tonight the familiarity is kinda comforting, like sliding into a pair of well-worn slippers. "Yes, ma'am."

The water's steamy hot, but no matter how much soap I use, it still feels like the entire forest is clinging to my skin. I change into my PJs and catch a glimpse of myself in the mirror. Fog clouds the glass so only a fuzzy version of me is visible. Like Bell in the whirlwind of white. I wipe my hand across the mirror. One minute he was full of spit and venom and the next he was sprawled out on the dirt. It wasn't right.

When I get to my room, the door's open and Ezra's sitting on my bed, arms crossed. "Hey."

"Hi." I dig my toes into the carpet. I want to tell Ezra that what happened was a big deal and I can't get it out of my head, but the words get all gunked up on their way to my mouth. Instead, I perch on the edge of my desk chair and stare at my feet.

"You okay? I kinda cleared out quick."

"I guess," I say. "Better than Bell anyway."

Ezra pulls one of my pillows against his chest. "It was pretty crazy out there."

Hearing him admit that tonight was messed up starts to loosen the tight knot inside me. "Ezra, can I ask you something?"

"What is it?"

"Bell said the woods weren't safe. Then later, he pulled you close and said something else. What was it?"

Ezra shrugs. "Just a bunch of gibberish."

"Like?"

He lifts his eyes to the ceiling as though he's trying hard to remember. "Oaf Yo . . . Core Dee Sups? Something like that."

"Oaf Yo Core Dee Sups?" I ask, making a mental note of the strange words.

"He wasn't making sense, Maggie. It could have been 'Old Fido's Corvette.'"

"Huh?"

"Like, if one of his dogs was named Fido and he wanted to leave it a fancy car in his will. Old people do weird stuff."

That's a dumb theory, but I don't have a better one, so I let it go. "I saw something. When he was coughing. Glowing dust came out of his mouth. Like a neon cloud."

"That whole forest was filled with glowing stuff," Ezra says.

"I know . . . but it got all over you."

Ezra gives me a sideways smile. "You're not worried about me, are you?"

I pull my knees to my chest. "Maybe."

"Being old isn't contagious, Mags. I'm gonna be fine." Ezra stands. "You should get some sleep."

"Yeah, you too."

When I'm alone again, I don't feel sleepy. My muscles are tight and my stomach squeezes in on itself. If I close my eyes now, I don't think I'll like what I imagine in the darkness. Instead, I reach for a worn leather journal on my nightstand and flip to a familiar page. The entry's dated January 4.

> I hit the road bright and early tomorrow morning. I've always dreamed of a chance like this—exploring the wilds, making discoveries. But that park ranger's cabin is going to be awfully lonely without Ezra and Maggie to fill it up.
> I know Ezra's having a rough time with me going. He would hardly look at me the last few days. But my little Magnolia, she's still buzzing around like always. Coming up with all sorts of plans of her own. I think she'll be okay until we're back together again. At least I hope so.

I hold the journal close. Dad's scratchy handwriting and a faded coffee ring make the pages feel alive, like a part of him is still living in Shady Pines. After he moved, I found it in a box with a few of his T-shirts. I asked him if he wanted us to mail it to Yellowstone, but he said I should keep it. So I have.

I breathe in the scent of leather and ink and finally flip to a blank page and grip my pen.

Field Observations
Bioluminescent fungi discovered in Old Man
   Bell's woods
Unexplained phenomenon: swirling white cloud,
   hum in trees, howling wind, glowing sparks
   coming from Old Man Bell

I close the book. None of it makes much sense right now. But as Gramma says, "Things always look brighter in the morning." I crawl into bed and pull the blankets over my head, forcing myself to squeeze my eyes shut.

Whispering branches, neon faces, and Old Man Bell's warnings slip in and out of my dreams.

CHAPTER SEVEN

R ise and shine, sleepyhead." Gramma stands in my
doorway decked out in magenta Bermuda shorts
and a matching polka-dot shirt. A purple fanny
pack is slung across her hips. "I'm heading into
town. If you want to come along, I'm leaving in five minutes."

My eyes skitter to Dad's camera propped up on my
desk. Applications for the Merit Award have to be postmarked by today. A big part of me thinks turning in last
night's photos is a slimy thing to do. Old Man Bell is
probably in the hospital right now, eating clear gelatin and
grumbling about how rotten kids are these days.

I chew my thumbnail. Then again, what's done is done.
This award is my one chance and I can't throw it away.

I hop out of bed and dig some mostly clean clothes out
of my hamper. A spotted lizard the size of my hand skitters across the terrarium. I pause and give Lennox a pinch
of dried crickets. "Bon appétit, buddy."

I rewind the film before popping it out of the camera—I learned the hard way not to skip that step—then dig into the mason jar on my desk. It's half-full of coins and bills from the nightcrawler worms I've sold down at the bait shop. I shove the cash and the film canister into my pocket and hustle to the living room.

Gramma gives me a once-over, then licks her thumb and swipes it across some stray hairs on my forehead.

I wriggle back. "Gramma! That's gross!"

"A little spit bath never hurt a soul. Now load up in the car if you're coming."

We park and walk along the downtown strip, passing Lou's Best Biscuits, First Gospel Church, and the Shady Pines Post Office. The sun beats down on the pavement, making heat waves in the air.

When we push through the glass doors at Goodman's Pharmacy, a pair of bells jingles. Gramma looks at her watch. "You can drop off your film, but I can't wait around until the pictures are ready. I've got yard work to tend to."

I drop the film in the one-hour developing slot and give a display of big, bright lollipops a spin. I used to be obsessed with these things and spend every spare quarter on them. Raspberry, cotton candy, green apple.

Neon blue. Day-Glo green.

As the display whirls, the fluorescent colors blur and the carousel gives a low squeal. I can almost hear a moan rolling down the toothpaste aisle. I yank back my hands and hurry off to find Gramma.

She stands in front of the cosmetics section holding two tubes of lipstick. "What do you think, flamingo jamboree or carnation kisses?"

I picture the bright shades smudged across Gramma's teeth or paired up with a matching fanny pack. "What about some nice ChapStick? It's got SPF and everything. Now that's what I call a quality lip product."

"Carnation kisses it is." Gramma drops the tube in the cart and wheels to the checkout. On the way, we pass a display of Vitaccino health drinks. A sign next to the cartons reads: VITACCINO'S PROPRIETY BLEND RELIEVES MUSCLE ACHES, FATIGUE, POOR SLEEP, AND SIGNS OF PREMATURE AGING. There's a picture of Dr. Lydia Croft in the bottom corner. She's got short, silvery hair like Gramma, but instead of polka dots and fuchsia lipstick, Dr. Croft wears pearl earrings and a gray blazer.

Gramma clucks her tongue. "That woman never gets tired of tooting her own horn. Thirty dollars for a six-pack of snake oil juice. Highway robbery is what I call it."

Gramma still hasn't forgiven the Crofts for firing Dad. I can't exactly blame her. I was mad at first too. But the more I thought about it, the more I realized we needed to spend our energy getting on their good side. After all, the Crofts are the only people in town with the power to rehire Dad. That's why this Merit Award is so important. Once I get in front of the board, I can explain that what happened in the lab was a one-time mix up. Dad might be a smidge scatterbrained, but he's still a genius. He knows more about rocks and bugs and stars and birds than anybody. I know he could be a huge help at Vitaccino if they'd just give him another shot.

Gramma and I grab our bags and head for the car. When we pass Lou's Best Biscuits, the door swings open. A mass of black and brown fur charges out. Three dobermans. I stumble into the hood of Gramma's car. It's Old Man Bell's dogs. The fur around their necks bristles as they sniff my legs.

"Since when are you scared of dogs, Magnolia?" Gramma reaches down and pats one of the dobermans. It wags its nub of a tail.

Sheriff Huxley and Deputy Ronald dash out of the diner and scramble for the dangling leashes. "Sorry about that, ladies. These dogs have minds of their own." The sheriff tilts his hat up. "Oh, it's you again. They must've smelled something familiar and wanted to say hello."

Gramma narrows her eyes. "Morning, sheriff."

Sweat prickles along the back of my neck. I look up at the sky. Maybe a lightning bolt or a hailstorm will zing down and end this little chat before somebody starts talking about glowing fungus or trespassing.

"We never got a chance to thank you proper for the heads-up last night. Course, you kids shouldn't have been around there in the first place, but under the circumstances, I'll let it slide." Sheriff Huxley gives a low whistle. "I hadn't been that way in ages. That place sure is a sight."

Gramma pivots toward the sheriff. "And what place would that be?"

The hailstorm is gonna be too late to save me. I slide off the hood of the Ford. "I sure am getting hungry, Gramma. I skipped breakfast and you know how growing kids—"

Gramma gives me a look that glues my tongue to the roof of my mouth.

"The woods outside town. Where the kids found Hiram Bell," the sheriff says with a sad frown. "We tried to resuscitate him, but it was too late. I guess it was the old feller's time to go."

My throat feels tight and achy. Old Man Bell didn't make it. He isn't eating Jell-O or calling his doctor a know-it-all whippersnapper. He's gone for good. I keep my eyes on my sneakers.

"Oh that," Gramma says. "Of course. Awful sad business."

I peek up at Gramma and finally understand why she brings in rolls of quarters every other week at the Raccoon Creek Poker Night. She can bluff like nobody's business.

"Our guess is it was a heart attack. But at his age, coulda

been anything." The sheriff gives the leashes a shake. "The department's adopting the pups. I think they'll make real fine officers, with a little training."

Deputy Ronald bends down and scratches one of the dogs behind the ear. It gives a low growl and the deputy jerks his hand back.

"That's right nice of you, boys. Well, we'd best be getting on now. What with Magnolia needing to catch up on her rest after such a trying night."

My palms are sweaty, and I desperately wish I could melt down the street grate and disappear like a puddle of goo.

Gramma swings my car door open and nods to my seat. "In you go, Magnolia Jane Stone."

I am the deadest girl in dead town.

CHAPTER EIGHT

We drive in silence, hitting reds at the only two stoplights in Shady Pines. When we pass the Thurston County Library, Gramma jerks the wheel, swerving into the parking lot. She spins toward me. "Spill your guts now, Magnolia. What in blue blazes were you doing out in those woods so late? And Hiram Bell died? When were you planning on telling me any of this?"

"I didn't know he died. I thought he was gonna be okay." I pick at the fraying edge of my cut-off shorts.

"What were you doing out there in the first place?"

"I needed a picture for the Merit Award and . . . the rest is kinda hard to explain."

"You'd better start trying." Gramma presses her fingers against her temples like she's fighting off the mother of all headaches.

I think back to the weird stuff we bumped into last night and decide it's best to go easy on the details. "I was snapping some pictures of the trees when Old Man Bell and his dogs showed up. He was yelling. Then he started coughing and then he just sorta fell down."

Gramma's eyes spark with curiosity, then spring back to rabid honey badger mode. "And you didn't think that was something you oughta share with me?"

"I figured you'd be mad."

"Course I'm mad. I don't wanna go finding out my family happenings from Sheriff Huxley."

I pull a loose thread from the fray of my shorts and twist it around my finger. I know Gramma probably wishes she could just garden or play bunco all day like other old ladies. Instead, she's got me and Ezra to worry about. And Ezra makes enough trouble for both of us. "I'm sorry. I should have told you."

"Darn right you should have." She shakes her head. "I don't mind you kids exploring. Back when I was your age, I roamed Shady Pines from sunup to sundown. But you gotta be smart about it. That means you don't go wandering after dark in spots with NO TRESPASSING signs. You understand what I'm saying?"

"Yes, Gramma. I'm sorry. Really."

She lets out a breath, and then her hands fall to her lap. "Anything else I oughta know?"

I could tell Gramma the whole truth. The fog rising from the ground. The neon dust. Bell's last words. It'd probably feel good to dump it off my chest. Then somebody else would be in charge of figuring out what it all meant. "I've never seen a person have a heart attack before."

Gramma eyes her reflection in the rearview mirror. In the morning sun, the lines around her mouth look deeper than usual. "Death's a hard thing to wrap your mind around. I remember the day Ernie passed like it was yesterday. We were tending to the azaleas in the front beds. Your daddy was toddling about in the shade. Then all of a sudden Ernie up and grabbed his chest, said, 'Trudi, I need to rest a spell.' Those were his last words. He's been resting out behind Good Servant Church ever since." Gramma blinks a few times and then clears her throat. "People up and die. And it's hardly ever good timing for the ones they leave behind."

I think about Gramma raising Dad all alone. How hard it must've been on both of them. "Did you ever feel mad that you lost Grandpa so young?"

"Sure I did. But then after a while I realized all that anger was making me forget about what I still had. Your daddy. Two working arms and a set of legs. A job that could pay the bills. Staying mad wouldn't put food on the table or keep the lights on." Gramma gazes toward the deep green pines that border the library. She's got a far-off look like she's traveled way back to the days when Dad was small and she was still young. But when she finally speaks again, her voice sounds the same as always. "I'm sorry that you had to be there when Bell passed. I reckon that was mighty frightening. Yet dying's a natural part of living. From dust to dust. Ashes to ashes."

Gramma's got sayings like that for just about everything. Sometimes they make me feel better, but mostly they leave me more confused. "What if Bell's death wasn't natural? Some people say those woods are haunted or cursed or—"

"Those woods are just woods. I know you're shook up, Magnolia, but the best thing is to keep on keeping on."

Gramma doesn't want to talk this out. She just wants me to settle down. I glance out my window. A black bird flutters to a puddle in the library parking lot. It wriggles its wings and dips its beak into the water. It's a great-tailed grackle. Dad once said they're some of the scrappiest birds he knows. They live all over the place. Eat just about anything. The bird tilts its head, peering over the hot asphalt with beady yellow eyes. It looks a little lost. Like maybe it planned to be scrappy, but then things happened and it forgot how.

Gramma gives me a long look and then pats my knee. "Death is scary and sad. I wish you hadn't bumped into it quite so early, but then life doesn't always go the way we'd like." Gramma reaches for one of the Goodman's sacks and pulls out a chocolate bar. She unwraps it and breaks the candy in two. "Have a bite. It'll make you feel better."

I shake my head. I can't eat sweets when I've still got wispy bits of forest floating around in my head.

Gramma munches on the chocolate and then tucks the other half into her fanny pack. She turns on the country music station and puts the car back into drive. Gramma sways her head to the music and I can tell she's given Bell's death all the thinking she plans to.

Back home Gramma whips up a stack of tuna melts and little cups of fruit cocktail. I pick at my food and scan the counter for Dad's journal. Whenever I can't get him on the phone or by e-mail, I can at least flip through his pages. I scoot away a bottle of Gramma's fiber pills and a stack of junk mail, but the book's not here.

"Gramma, did you move Dad's journal?"

"Don't think so," Gramma calls from the living room recliner.

I search around the computer and under the desk. "I had it yesterday, and now it's gone."

Gramma turns the volume up on her soap opera. "It's bound to be around somewhere."

I've flipped through that journal nearly every day since Dad moved. It's loaded with his goofy drawings, scribbled notes, and old to-do lists. I can't lose it.

I jog down the hall and tear through my room. I check every drawer, dusty corner, and even under the bed. Nothing.

I peek down the hall. Ezra's door is cracked open and rock music with whiny singing drifts out.

I tap on the door. "Ezra?"

There's no answer.

I glance over my shoulder, then push my foot into the gap. There's a wad of candy wrappers on his desk and the place smells like imitation evergreen from the body spray he's always squirting.

I peek under his bed. A rusty silver bucket with a bit of dirt trickling down the side lurks in the shadows. I narrow my eyes. If Ezra's plotting to take over selling night-crawler worms to the bait shop, he can think again. That gig is mine. I reach for the bucket, not entirely sure if I'm planning to confiscate it or leave him a warning note telling him to back off.

That's when I see it. The edge of Dad's journal pokes out from inside the bucket. There're smudges of mud across the cover. I snatch it. If Ezra had asked to borrow it, that'd be one thing. But this? Stealing it and then dumping it in some cruddy pail? Ultra-rude.

I storm out of Ezra's room, slamming the door behind me.

I flop on my bed and flip through the journal, wiping off bits of dried dirt as I go. I stop. In the middle, there's rough edges where several sheets have been torn out. I run my fingers down the ragged pages. Spray-painting some trees is one thing; messing with Dad's journal is a whole other level of rotten. Especially after what happened last night.

As I rehearse all the words I'm gonna hurl at Ezra the next time I see him, the cuckoo clock in the living room chirps twelve times.

Noon. The mailman will be here in two hours.

I slide the journal between my mattress and my box spring. If I'm going to get my Merit Award application in on time, I'll have to save strangling Ezra for later. I grab my backpack, wave to Gramma, and race out the door. I ring the bell at Nate's place, and he answers in three seconds flat. The TV blares cartoons and Nate's three-year-old twin brothers, Collin and Benny, are arguing about whose turn it is to hold the remote.

"I've gotta pick up my film at Goodman's. Wanna—"

"Yup." Nate scrambles down the porch and then yells over his shoulder. "Going out with Mags. Be back later."

At the photo counter, I slap down five dollars for the pictures.

Kiki, the cashier with frizzy blond hair and braces, chews on a wad of pink gum. "Those are some weird-looking pictures you got there."

There's no such thing as privacy in a small town. "It's science stuff." I give Kiki a mind-your-own-beeswax kinda look and hustle down the aisles in search of Nate. When I find him, he's got a huge, bright orange squirt gun propped against his shoulder.

"Looks fancy," I say.

"It's the MegaBlaster 3000. Targeting scope. Blasts up to forty feet, and when the crossbow's deployed it can shoot three separate streams. This is the mother of all squirt guns."

I eye the twenty-five-dollar price tag. "You got any money?"

"Two bucks in nickels at home . . . but when you win that award we'll have enough."

I'd planned to use any winnings on something scientific. Like a microscope or fancy binoculars but with this heat, an epic water fight sounds pretty amazing. "Totally, and enough for those water grenades, too."

"Pew, pew, pew." Nate pumps the MegaBlaster's trigger. "You really think you can get the board to rehire your dad?"

"Dad's the smartest guy I know. They'd be crazy to not give him another shot."

Nate shrugs. "My dad said rich people are hard to figure out."

"It'll all come together. You'll see."

Nate puts the MegaBlaster 3000 back on the shelf. "Until later, Oh Great King of the Squirt Guns."

Back at Raccoon Creek, we climb the clubhouse ladder and smoosh down into our beanbag chairs. I tear into the photo envelope.

I grin. They turned out good. Fleshy mushrooms shine atomic green against a backdrop of velvety black forest. I flip through a few more pictures and then stop at one of the landscape shots. In the background near the dark outline of trees, there's a blur of white.

The hair at the back of my neck rises. The fuzzy cloud has a shape. Head, shoulders, legs.

CHAPTER NINE

Nate leans in. "Whoa, what the heck is that?"

After last night, the last thing I need is to throw Nate into full-blown paranormal investigator mode. I flip to the next photo. "Lens was probably dirty."

"The old dirty lens theory." Nate shakes his head. "Some people might buy that sort of thing, but I know aliens when—"

"Nate!" A voice hollers from the ground, saving me from another of Nate's UFO speeches. We poke our heads out the clubhouse window. Nate's dad stands on the gravel drive wearing a greasy mechanic's uniform. The twins are wrapped around his legs. "I'm taking an extra shift down at the shop. I need ya to watch the boys."

"I wanna Popsicle and a bubble bath!" Collin whines, his red curls jutting out every which way.

Nate shakes his head gravely. "Babysitting is the bane of my existence."

I crack a smile. "How much longer till your mom gets back from Georgia?"

"Like, a month. All because twins run in the family. Apparently, they're even harder to take care of as squishy little newborns. At least that's the story my aunt Josie's telling."

"Hustle up, Nate. I got work!" Nate's dad calls.

"I'll catch you later, Mags." Nate trudges down the ladder. The boys peel off their dad and onto Nate. "Two orange Popsicles coming up."

"I wanna purple 'sicle," Benny whines.

"No! I wanna purple." Collin shoves Benny and they both start to howl.

"Have fun," I call, and then grab a manila envelope tucked under a stack of old *Nat Geo* magazines. My application for the Merit Award has been printed for days, just waiting for me to fill in the blanks describing my photos. I carefully print a few lines about the mushrooms and the wonders of bioluminescence. After that, I add a final bit about Dad teaching me almost everything I know about the flora and fauna of Shady Pines.

I slide in two of the best photographs—close-ups of a brilliant turquoise mushroom—then trot to the row of mailboxes at the entrance to Raccoon Creek. I close my eyes and drop the letter in the chute. I'm inching my way toward that award.

I step inside the trailer just as the phone rings, and nearly trip over Ezra's skateboard racing to answer it.

"Magnolia?" The voice sounds far away, like the call's coming from somewhere deep underground.

"Dad?" I spin in a circle wrapping the cord around my chest.

"Hi, kid! It's me."

"You've got service!"

"My supervisor's visiting my campsite and has a satellite phone. I sorta borrowed it while he went to check on a troop of Cub Scouts."

Sizzle.

Pop!

"What's all that?"

"I'm working on a little something. I know a special lady who just turned eleven."

"My birthday was last month, Dad. And you already mailed me a card and sang me happy birthday in your goofy British accent."

"That wasn't British, my lady. T'was Scottish," he says, swinging into the bad imitation again. "But I still owe you a present. So I wanted to see about your favorite color these days. And if you prefer transparent or opaque. Hypothetically speaking, of course. No spoilers."

Crackle.

Bang!

"Whoa there. Easy does it."

"Are you doing something dangerous?" I want to update Dad on everything that happened in the woods, but it sounds like he's in the middle of a potential catastrophe.

"What? No, kiddo. Just tinkering around a bit. You know me. Having a little fun before work."

"There's no smoke or anything, right?"

Dad coughs. "I'd say it's more of a mist, really. Low-hanging sulfuric cloud, possibly."

"Dad! Yellowstone has rules about that sorta thing. You could get in trouble!"

"No worries, Magaroni and Cheese. I'm at a campfire in a designated area. Plus, I've got two fire extinguishers on hand if need be." He coughs. "Everything is one hundred percent under control."

Sizzle, snap . . . crackle.

"Ouch! Okay . . . um, actually, I'd better run . . . so did you say green was a good color for you? Things are looking a bit green."

"Green's great."

"Perfect. Listen, I'm going to be out of range for another week or so, but you keep checking the mail, okay?"

There's a sound like a giant pot of pasta sauce boiling over.

"Sure, Dad. Just get the fire put out."

"No problemo. I've got this under—"

"Tooooommmy!" A man's voice hollers.

"Love you, kid—"

The line goes dead.

I set the phone back on the receiver. I'm going to need to get in front of the Vitaccino board stat. It sounds like Dad may need a new job sooner than expected.

CHAPTER TEN

I lay back on my bed and flip through the rest of the pictures. I pause. There's one I didn't notice before. It must've been taken by accident when we were running. It's a little hazy, but one of the doberman's faces is completely in focus. Something pokes out of its mouth—long, skinny, and white—like a bean sprout in the chicken chow mein at Eggroll King.

I open my nightstand drawer and dig out my magnifying glass. Enlarged, it looks like the white stalk is actually attached to the dog's bottom lip. I didn't notice anything on the dogs this morning, but then again, there wasn't really time to examine them while Sheriff Huxley was ratting me out to Gramma.

There's a tap at my door, and I shove the photos under my pillow. The door creaks open and Ezra hovers in the entry. "Hey."

I purse my lips. "Are you here to apologize for vandalizing Dad's journal?"

"Huh?" Ezra barely blinks.

"You tore pages out. What kind of creepazoid does that?"

"I didn't tear anything out. I just looked at it. You shouldn't go snooping around in my room anyway."

"You left the door open."

"Well, you left the notebook on the counter. So we're even." Ezra leans against the doorjamb like destruction of personal property is no big deal.

I punch my pillow. "Those pages didn't just pull themselves out!"

"Maybe they got stuck on something sticky and it yanked them out."

I roll my eyes. That totally didn't happen. But I don't have enough evidence to keep arguing, so I decide to let it go for now. Ezra lingers in the doorway. "Did you want something?"

He sighs, then shoves his hands into his pockets. "Thanks for not ratting me out to Gramma when you got busted."

"I figure she didn't need to know every detail," I say. Ezra and I might not always get along, but I'm not one to snitch unless I have to.

"She told me you guys bumped into the sheriff. She said Old Man Bell died."

A snapshot of Bell's glowing face flashes through my mind and I shudder. "Heart attack."

"That's messed up. I wish I coulda helped him more."
He fiddles with the hem of his black T-shirt. "Anyway, I
wanted to make sure you were okay and stuff."

"I guess. You?"

"Yeah. I just thought—" Ezra's words suddenly die off
in a fit of coughing.

His face gets a greenish tint. Like he ate too many fried
Twinkies at the county fair. At last, Ezra wipes his eyes
and sputters out, "I think I'm allergic to your cat."

"Um . . . okay." We've had Pascal since he was a kitten
and Ezra's never so much as sniffled around him.

"I just thought I'd check on you. That's all." Ezra turns
and goes. Faint coughing drifts down the hall after him.

Brothers are weird. One minute I want to sock him in
the nose for being a stinkface and the next I kinda want
to hug him.

I'm reaching for the photos under my pillow when
something rustles in the corner of the room. I glance up
to see Lennox hurl his little lizard body against his terrarium glass. He pounces again, this time tumbling backward onto his heating rock. "You're going to shed your tail
if you keep freaking out."

I pop the lid off and scoop him out. As soon as he's
free, he leaps to my arm, then scrambles down my leg
onto the carpet. I drop to my knees. I'm inches from
grabbing him when he springs across the room as fast as

a four-inch leopard gecko can possibly run.

"You're being a psychopath," I yell and dash after him.

There's a meow, and I whirl around. Pascal saunters into the room like a lion creeping through the African savanna. I spread my arms wide. Pascal's tail twitches as Lennox races up the back wall and disappears behind the curtains.

Pascal crouches to pounce. "You CANNOT eat my lizard!" I swoop down and grab Pascal around the middle. He gives a sulky cry as I toss him out and slam my bedroom door.

I throw my curtains back, but there's no sign of Lennox. "Come here, boy. You're safe now." I reach for the miniblinds cord and give it a tug.

"Whoa."

On the other side of the window, three massive spiders creep along an intricate web. They're the size of my fist, with dazzling yellow stripes running down each side of their bulging black abdomens.

Lennox opens his mouth and runs in the direction of a wriggling leg. "They're as big as you. Not a good snack."

I normally don't mind bugs, but a gang of overgrown arachnids boogying on my windowsill is pushing it. I give the web a sideways glance. A distinct zigzag pattern runs down the center. I know the species that makes it—yellow garden spiders, a kind of orb-weaver. I've accidentally walked into their webs a bunch of times. Only these guys look like they've been pumping some serious iron.

As they add more silky strands to their web, I remember another fact about orb-weavers.

They always hunt alone.

I grab Lennox and plop him back in the terrarium. There's gotta be a scientific explanation for the arachnid dance party outside my window. Maybe it's some kind of mating ritual or a defense mechanism for scaring away predators.

I walk back to the window as a dragonfly glides by. Its wings barely brush the sticky web and the spiders spring to action, charging the center of the web and shooting out strand after strand of silvery thread. In less than ten seconds, the dragonfly is bound tight in a coil of deadly silk.

My breath catches as the dragonfly's head gives a final twitch before disappearing in white. Maybe I've somehow got the species wrong or maybe this particular group is really good at being team players. I snag the magnifying glass from my nightstand and hold it over a particularly large specimen. It's got eight long, jointed legs, and a bulging black abdomen. All normal.

But there's still something off about these guys. I grab the mason jar filled with my nightcrawler cash, dump it, and head for the front door. First, there was the bumblebee moth and then the doberman. Now these spiders. Strange critters are scooting around Shady Pines, and it's my scientific duty to find out why.

CHAPTER ELEVEN

The web stretches from the top of my window all the way to the ledge. It's easily the biggest, thickest one I've ever seen. And the spiders creep out from the center in slow, orderly steps. Like they're all part of some spidery cuckoo clock that rotates them automatically.

I hold the mason jar under the wriggling web. When it touches their silk, the spiders launch toward my hand. A hulking one with an abdomen the size of a walnut reaches the jar first. It plunks to the bottom then starts to scuttle back up the glass. Before it can make a getaway, I screw the lid on tight.

Back inside, I grab a butcher knife and head to my room. I poke three holes in the lid for air. The spider's spindly legs tink against the glass.

It crawls up the side of the jar then slips down. I glance to the window. The spiders outside climb up their web then glide down. I give the jar a little shake and the captured spider scurries in a circle. Along the web, the remaining two race around like they're running laps at track.

These guys are seriously weird. I grab a pen and reach for the journal.

Spiders Exhibit Strange Characteristics
Larger than average size
Hanging out in a group instead of alone
Synchronized movements

I once read a *Nat Geo* article about hive mind. Creatures like ants, birds, and fish use it to organize activity in their groups. But these spiders aren't even together anymore and they're still pulling off a choreographed routine. If I could figure out why, that would really be something worth telling the Vitaccino board about.

I snap a few photos, including a close-up of the mummified dragonfly. I'm adjusting the lens when the floorboard in the hall creaks. It only makes that sound when someone's trying hard to be stealthy.

I poke my head out the door and catch Ezra slinking by. He's traded his usual skinny jeans and sneakers for rain boots and baggy cargo shorts.

"What are you doing?"

"Nothing." He gives me an innocent blink that might fool Gramma but only confirms he's up to no good.

"Do you always wear rain boots when you're doing nothing?"

"What? I've got some stuff to do outside."

The only thing Ezra ever does outside is skateboard and those boots would be a sure way to bust an ankle. I've got a powerful feeling Ezra's planning something really dumb. "Please tell me you're not going back there."

"Shhhhh." He peeks down the hall. Twangy country music drifts from Gramma's partially open door. "Maybe I am. So what?"

"But why?"

Ezra's eyes are glassy like he's fighting off a bad cold. "I had some crazy dreams last night. I kept seeing Bell. He was screaming at the trees. Like he actually expected someone to answer him. And now that I know he died, I need to go back. See the place again in the daytime."

"The sheriff might still be hanging around. You could get in trouble."

"I can't explain it, Mags, but I have to do this." Ezra pauses. "You could come with me. Get some more pictures or whatever."

I chew my lip. Part of me wants to stuff my feet into sneakers and tag along. I can't even remember the last time Ezra invited me to do something with him.

"Come on, Mags. Live a little." Ezra gives me a half smile.

A creeping feeling skates up my spine. I haven't forgotten the murmurs in the woods or the way the dogs ran scared to Old Man Bell. Going back there is a bad idea. "How about a movie instead? I could make some extra-buttery popcorn."

Ezra's smile crumples. "Forget it." He heads for the door without another word.

I lean against the doorframe, feeling an achy pang in my chest. Even if it's a dumb move, Ezra's still my brother and I don't like the idea of him out there alone. Before I can trot out the door after him, Gramma sashays out of her bedroom in her white cook's uniform. She glances toward the front door. "I suppose Ezra's gone gallivanting around town without worrying about doing any chores?"

"Something like that."

Gramma tilts her wrist and glances at her watch. "Well, I've gotta be making my way to Sunny Day for the evening shift. I'm leaving a cheeseburger pie in the fridge for dinner. Twenty minutes at three-fifty. And while I'm thinking of it, could you take out the trash? The kitchen's starting to smell like a kitty litter and banana peel sandwich."

I sneak a look out the front window. Ezra's just about to go over the hill and out of sight. "Could I do it later?"

She crosses her arms over her chest. "Chores make your bones grow stronger. Now hop to it."

I sigh. "Yes, ma'am."

By the time I'm done, it'll be too late to catch up with Ezra. I've just gotta hope that he doesn't do anything too stupid while he's there. Which is basically the same thing as hoping for a miracle.

CHAPTER TWELVE

I glance out my window. The sun hovers low in the sky, casting rays of orange and raspberry sherbet over my bedspread. Ezra called a few minutes ago and said he was staying the night at Zion's. I asked him what he did in the woods, but all he said was, "Not much." Typical Ezra.

Even after scouring my collection of science magazines and scanning oodles of online nature articles, I couldn't find anything about orb-weavers forming a hunting party.

I mosey to the living room and click on the TV. A *Medical Mysteries* rerun is on. It's about a marathon runner who started hearing a weird buzzing in her chest. Then she got a cough. It turned out she'd inhaled a beetle and the thing was stuck in her lung. I peer down the dark hall. Ezra hasn't sucked in any bugs, but a mouthful of spores might not be much better.

I turn the TV off and head down the hall. Ezra's door is shut but there's a low hum coming from inside. I slink in as silent as a world-class sneak.

The room's muggy—the way the shower feels after I've let the steam build up too much. The humidifier Gramma gets out when we have colds gyrates in a slow circle on Ezra's desk. The trailer's already too hot and sticky without Ezra making things worse. I turn it off and scan the rest of the room. Something shiny pokes out from behind his blinds. I pull the cord, hoping I'm not gonna bump into another mondo web. Instead, there's a layer of aluminum foil spread across the glass, blocking out every last scrap of daylight. Ezra's probably trying to be all cool and rock-star-like with a dark, dreary room.

I shut the blinds and peek under his bed. The rusty silver bucket I spotted earlier is gone but there's a fuzzy green circle and a musty smell in its place.

"Ew." Brothers are disgusting.

I shut the door and head back to the living room. I pour myself a glass of sweet tea and grab Dad's journal, flipping through some of my latest entries.

Field Observations

Bioluminescent fungi inhabit Old Man Bell's woods

Spiders show signs of hive mind

Then in smaller letters down at the bottom of the page:

Oaf Yo Core Dee Sups

Old Man Bell's last words. I'd sorta forgotten about them, with everything else going on. My eyes slide to the swirling blue lights of the computer's screen saver. It seems like a long shot that a bit of gibberish will help, but like Dad says, "You'll never know unless you try."

I type "Oaf Yo Core Dee Sups."

Ads for surfboards and websites in other languages load.

I try "Ofio Core Di Seps."

More random web pages.

I take a gulp of tea and give it a last-ditch effort. "Ofio Cordi Ceps."

The results load and the tea makes a wrong turn in my windpipe. Beneath a couple of ads, there's a photo of a mangled ant covered in gnarly white fuzz. It's got a skinny stalk poking up from the top of its head. "Ophiocordyceps Infects South American Carpenter Ants."

I peer down at my notes. Oaf Yo Core Dee Sups. And then back at the screen. Ophio-cordy-ceps.

That's too close to be a coincidence.

I click the link and more pictures load. In every one, the same dusty stalk sprouts out of an ant's head. There's something strangely familiar about it all. I flip a few pages back in my notebook. There's an entry on the bumblebee moth with the third antenna and the doberman with the bean sprout growth.

Stalks, antennas, bean sprouts. The first inklings of a crazy hypothesis are churning in my head.

I read down the page.

"Using a cocktail of toxins, Ophiocordyceps takes over the carpenter ant's central nervous system. As the fungus spreads, a stroma stalk filled with spores forms. Because of its ability to control its host's mind, Ophiocordyceps has been dubbed the zombie ant fungus."

ZOMBIE ANT FUNGUS.

I feel like Nate's somehow hacked my computer and shoved this article straight to my screen. I click on a photo of an ant hanging upside down on a leaf. Its body is shriveled and totally gunked up with a thick layer of white fuzz. Its mouthparts lock into the leaf as it gets ready to release gazillions of spores on its fellow ants. "The fungus compels its hosts to infect countless others and thrives in the humid climate of the rain forest."

That's messed up. Even for nature.

The ant's cloudy eyes stare at me through the screen. The stalks are bad enough, but the thought of these ants turning on their own colonies is brutal.

Worst of all, this stuff might be cropping up in Shady Pines.

I click on an image of the spore stalk under a microscope. It fans out wide like some exotic poisonous jellyfish. I sketch the shape in Dad's journal, wondering how the stuff could've made it all the way to our little town.

Pascal waltzes into the room from some hidden corner where he's probably been snoozing and dreaming of shredding giant dust bunnies. He weaves his way to the front door and lets out a loud meow.

"It's late," I say. "You can roam tomorrow."

He pokes out his claws and makes a single scratch mark across the door.

"Pascal! Do you want Gramma to kill me?" I hurry over and crack the door wide enough for him to slip out. "Make it snappy."

His tail swishes as he drifts into the darkness. A faint light flashes nearby, a firefly maybe. I take a tiny step out onto the porch. Pascal's already in full prowl mode, his head ducking low as he stalks something in the grass.

He darts forward. Two small circles gleam from the lawn. Then another pair and another. Six shining green orbs blink up at me.

CHAPTER THIRTEEN

There's a hiss and then a throaty growl, but it isn't Pascal who's in a tizzy. It's a mother opossum with two gerbil-size babies clinging to her back.

Two trailers down, branches rattle and a dark mass shifts. It's something way bigger than these rope-tailed marsupials.

"Pascal, get back here!" I scramble down the porch steps.

There's a crunch of gravel underfoot, then the shadow moves into the glow of Nate's porch light.

"Ezra! What are you doing out here? I thought you were staying at Zion's."

He shrugs. "Changed my mind."

The mother opossum peels back her lip and hisses before skulking away. Ezra stuffs his hands in his pockets, not even glancing in its direction. There's dirt smudged across his cargo shorts and his arms are streaked with green.

"So, are you gonna tell me what you really did at Bell's place?"

"Just looked around," Ezra answers, then his chest shakes as a hacking fit comes over him. When he finishes, he looks wiped out. "Why are you staring at me like that?"

"You're coughing again."

"People cough. It's not a big deal." Ezra wipes a hand across his mouth. His fingers glow dimly blue.

Ezra shouldn't be coughing, or glowing, or sneaking around Old Man Bell's creepy woods. "I figured out what Bell was trying to tell us. It wasn't anything about Old Fido's Corvette. It was Ophiocordyceps."

"Huh?"

"It's a parasitic fungus that takes over ants' minds and makes them infect their own colonies." I bite my lip. This is the part where things get a little iffy. "They call it the zombie ant fungus, but I'm pretty sure it's infecting other species in Shady Pines. Moths, dogs. Maybe other stuff too."

Ezra gives a lifeless laugh. "You've been spending way too much time with Nate. Zombies are in movies, not real life."

"This fungus is the real deal, Ezra."

"Do we really need to talk about this right now? I'm tired. Plus, you sound like a crazy person."

Ezra looks more than tired. He looks like he needs a giant bottle of vitamin C and a weeklong nap.

And then it hits me.

What if this jungle fungus doesn't just infect animals? What if . . .

Ezra tries to scoot past me, but I stretch out both arms, blocking his path. "Bell was coughing a ton that night. Then he died. And you breathed in a bunch of the glowing stuff from him."

"Mags, come on. I'm not infected with some zombie fungus."

I cross my arms. "You can't go back there."

"You can't tell me what to do. I've got my own plans and they're just as important as yours."

I scrunch my nose. "I'm trying to bring Dad home. All you've been doing is slinking around town making trouble."

Pascal emerges from the honeysuckle bush and twirls himself around my ankles. He peers up at Ezra, then pins his ears back and gives a low hiss.

Ezra frowns. "If Dad wanted to move back, he'd have done it by now."

"It's not that easy. There aren't a ton of jobs around here."

"Dad was ready to leave Shady Pines way before he got fired."

"Shady Pines is his home," I say, feeling my throat clench up the way it always does when Ezra starts in on Dad.

"It's also a little dump of a town with nothing but trees and bugs."

"We're here. That's not nothing."

Ezra stares at the trailer's aluminum roof like it's who he's been talking to all along. "Dad always wanted to see the world. To discover stuff nobody else had. Now he's surrounded by geysers and wolves and all sorts of wild things. You really think he's gonna come running back to Raccoon Creek Trailer Park?"

"He'll be back. You'll see." Ezra's wrong about Dad. He's wrong about everything.

"Think what you want." He stomps up the porch steps. "I'm going to bed."

A cloud passes over the moon and the night feels darker than ever, like morning may decide not to come around at all.

I trudge to my room and give the mason jar with the oversize orb-weaver a little shake. It skitters around the jar on long, dark legs. I remember the synchronized dance it did with its spider clan on the window. Ophiocordyceps might explain their hive mind. I find the photo of the doberman and rest it against the mason jar. They're the best evidence I've got that something strange is happening in Shady Pines.

If my hypothesis is right, this is a serious problem. A fungus that can turn creatures into spore-shooting zombies would be beyond dangerous. Especially if it's mutated and spreading to new species.

I flip to a blank page in Dad's journal.

> Action Plan for Tackling Possible Mutant Fungus Invasion
> Step One: Keep Ezra away from Bell's place until further notice.
> Step Two: Observe the spider for signs of infection.
> Step Three: Present findings to the board.

I pull my sheet up to my chin and close my eyes, waiting for sleep to wipe away the day.

Words bumble around in my head. Mind-controlled ants. Ezra. The woods.

Zombies.

CHAPTER FOURTEEN

hen I wake up, my room is bright and blazing hot. I toss off my sheet and grab the journal. I've got a lot to do, starting with keeping tabs on the captured orb-weaver. I snag a pen and hurry to my desk. But when I get there, all I find is an empty jar. My eyes dart side to side, and I half wonder whether the spider's pals let him out in the middle of the night. But arachnids don't have opposable thumbs. My face flushes hot. No-good, dirty, rotten older brothers do.

I storm down the hall, empty jar in hand. "Where's my spider?"

Gramma and Ezra sit at the kitchen table, smiling and quietly chatting. A swirl of steam rises from Gramma's coffee mug. She reaches over and pats Ezra's hand.

My eyes narrow to slits. "What's going on in here?"

Gramma chuckles. "Somebody got up on the wrong side of the bed. But you won't spoil my good mood, not when I've got a grandson who's turning into such a fine young man."

"What are you talking about?" Ezra hasn't done anything fine lately. Unless Gramma considers stealing other people's research projects and being a general pigheaded toot praiseworthy.

"Only thirteen and already gainfully employed. That's what I call taking responsibility."

"Ezra got a job?" My eyes snap to Ezra. "If you think you can steal my worm business—"

"I'm not selling any worms. Vitaccino hired me to help out around their plant." Ezra pokes at a plate of scrambled eggs with his fork.

"You've gotta be kidding me." I squeeze the mason jar between my palms.

"It's no joke." He shrugs. "They hired Jack and Zion, too."

"After what they did to your daddy, I'm not too fond of the Crofts myself, but I'm certainly not gonna stand in Ezra's way of earning some money this summer."

First the spider and now this. Ezra is trying to sabotage me. He knows I'm working to win the Merit Award and get in front of the board. But if he does something stupid at Vitaccino, all my plans for bringing Dad back will crumble. I spin to Gramma. "He can't work there. Tell him he has to find a job someplace else."

"What's gotten into you, Magnolia? You're getting all hot and bothered over nothing."

"It's not nothing. Ezra makes trouble wherever he goes." I glare at the empty jar, remembering everything Ezra said about Dad last night. "The only reason he's doing this is to mess things up for Dad. That's why he stole my spider. He's out to get me."

"Now, you need to calm down, Magnolia Jane. That's no way to talk about your brother. And besides, he didn't take your spider, I did."

"What?" I ask, feeling like somebody just sucker-punched me in the gut.

"I grabbed your hamper this morning and saw the vile thing scuttling all about. I didn't want it mucking up my good jar."

"I needed that spider—I'm doing important research!"

"I told you she's been moody about everything lately," Ezra says, giving Gramma a knowing look.

"I'm not moody!" I stomp one foot.

"I see." Gramma takes a long swig of coffee. "Why don't you have a seat and I'll make you a fried egg and cup of hot cocoa?"

"I don't want to sit down. Why can't Ezra collect cans or do a lemonade stand or something?"

"I'm thirteen. I'm not doing a lemonade stand."

"I've spent half the summer working for this Merit Award and Ezra's going to—"

"That's enough. You can have your opinions, but you

can't go hollering at your brother about a fine opportunity to make some money." Gramma stands and takes her mug to the sink. "Now if you'll excuse me, I've got errands to run before work."

"But Gramma—"

"I've heard all I want to. You and your brother need to get along. You're family. You gotta root for each other. Besides, nobody likes a sourpuss."

Gramma doesn't get it. This was our one shot to bring Dad home again. I slump down on a lumpy couch cushion.

"Oh, and one more thing." Gramma pauses at the front door. "I saw in the paper that there's going to be a memorial service for Hiram Bell. I think it'd be real nice if we made a showing."

I nod, but barely look up at Gramma. As she steps out the door, Ezra's eyes twinkle as they slide to mine. "Sorry I can't stay and chat. I've gotta get ready for work."

I hurl a fringed pillow at his head, but he dodges it and slinks to his room.

This is far from over.

I march down the hall and slam my bedroom door. I yank off my nightgown and grab the Yellowstone National Park T-shirt Dad sent last month. When I pull it over my head, the sleeves pinch me under the arms and the hem barely hits my belly button. It's at least two sizes too small.

Heat splotches my cheeks. If Dad were here, he'd know I hit a growth spurt. He'd know a lot of things.

I pull the shirt off and launch it across the room. It lands in a crumpled wad. I sink to the floor and stick my head between my knees. My nose drips and my eyes sting.

When I was little, I thought I'd have the world totally figured out once I hit double digits. But the questions keep growing. Like why everything that was good had to change. Why one mistake sent Dad across the country and left me here without him.

A gloomy, gray wave rolls over me. What if Ezra's right? What if I can't bring Dad home and things are this way forever? Dad a thousand miles away, never pointing out Venus in the night sky or laughing over Pascal ambushing his own tail. Drifting further and further apart until one day he doesn't even remember my middle name or my favorite ice cream.

A tear slips down my nose and a prickly feeling creeps up from somewhere deep inside. I imagine calling Dad. Shouting at him that he never should have gone to Yellowstone. Telling him that he's just like Mom. That I'll never forgive him.

But as the images stream through my mind, I see Dad. His shoulders slumped. The pain in his eyes. And I pull it all back in. I don't want to hurt him. I just want him home again.

I stand and pull a blue shirt dotted with tiny pink flowers over my head, then fold the Yellowstone T-shirt and put it back in the drawer. I don't know the answers. All I have is my plan. I've gotta hope that'll be enough.

If a mutated fungus really is spreading through Shady Pines, that's huge news. It might even be enough to wow the board into rehiring Dad, no matter what Ezra does. But I'll need some seriously stupendous evidence if I'm gonna prove it.

I grab some supplies and head out the door. Before I've even made it to Nate's front porch, the wispy little hairs around my face are glued to my skin. I ring the bell, and the sound of squealing toddlers erupts from inside. The door opens, and Benny—though it may in fact be his twin, Collin—stands in the doorway in an oversize cowboy hat, Spider-Man underwear, and swim flippers. "Hi, Magnowia."

"Hey, bud," I say, remaining name-neutral. "Nate around?"

He squints up at me. "How much will you give me if I tell ya?"

A bead of sweat glides down my neck. "Um . . . I was kind of hoping it might be free this time."

The twin giggles maniacally, then shrieks, "Nate! Magnowia's here! But you can't see her unless you pay me quarters!"

Nate appears a second later and gives the twin a shove out of the way. "Sorry, Collin's training to be a mobster. He won't do anything for free anymore. Wanna come in?"

"Actually, I wanted to see if you were up for a little sleuthing around town." I lower my voice and add, "There've been some developments in the last few hours. I need to brief you, stat."

"I'm always up for recon work," Nate says, grabbing his Darth Vader ball cap. "I'm heading out with Maggie. Be back later," he shouts over his shoulder.

Nate's dad calls out something resembling, "Have fun, you two," but the "Thomas the Tank Engine" theme song drowns him out.

"So what kind of developments are we talking about?" Nate asks as we pedal out of Raccoon Creek Trailer Park.

I meet his eye. "Brace yourself, this is big-time." I tell him everything—the spiders, the doberman, Ezra's symptoms, and the zombie-ant fungus.

"Whoa. That's mega-huge."

"I think Old Man Bell was trying to warn us that night. He knew the forest was loaded with the stuff."

Nate meets my eye with the kind of gloomy expression he saves for really rotten news, like when Lenny's Supermarket quit carrying Flamin' Hot Cheezy Poppers. "You said the gunk might be spreading around town making zombies, right? And Ezra got pretty close to Old Man

Bell, and now he's got the cough and the glow. So, not to freak you out or anything, but this is pretty much standard zombie apocalypse stuff."

I chew my lip. This time science sorta agrees with Nate. "Just keep pedaling."

CHAPTER FIFTEEN

Hours later, we coast down a hill and cruise along Maple Street. My eyes drift to the little blue house that used to be ours. Only the grass is too long and there's a plastic garden gnome knocked over in the front flower bed. Even the white minivan parked out front is all wrong. Nate glances my way. "You wanna stop and investigate? Maybe we could take a ride on the tire swing out back . . . if it's still there."

Nothing is the same anymore. Without Dad, our old place is just another house. "Nah, I'm good."

Sweat runs down my back and the buzz of cicadas blares from the trees. After a few more minutes of riding, there's the familiar sound of splashing and squealing. Like a June bug to a porch light, Nate instantly veers off the road toward the Shady Pines city pool.

Shouts of "Marco . . . Polo" drift from the water. Nate sighs. "Do you think those kids know they're living the dream?"

"We're on the hunt to solve a massive mystery and possibly make scientific history. Swimming can't compare to that kind of glory," I say, as a girl cannonballs into the shimmery blue water and another thick bead of sweat rolls down my neck.

"I'm just saying we've been searching around town for clues all day and haven't found anything. Maybe we'd think better after some splashing."

"We don't even have our suits."

Nate gives me an even more pitiful sigh. "My life's a wasteland of annihilated dreams."

A breeze ruffles my ponytail and I glance toward Nate with a sniff. A pungent odor slinks through the air. Nate sniffs too and then gives me an offended look. "Don't try to pin that stench on me. That doesn't even smell human."

I look over my shoulder to see if we've accidently pulled up near the dumpster, but there's only shrubs and mulch.

Nate slinks along the side of the pool, nose poking out like a bloodhound. "It's coming from over here."

I follow after him and stop when a horrible stink crashes into my nostrils. A rocket-shaped mushroom with a slimy film coating sprouts up from the grass. Flies buzz around the top of the tall dark stalk. I duck my nose into my T-shirt. It smells worse than a kitty litter and banana peel sandwich.

"The bugs are going nuts over it," Nate says as a wasp

lands next to a fly, seeming nearly glued on. "Don't they know when something stinks you clear out?"

"Flies like nasty stuff," I say, watching as several more buzz by. "So the more the mushroom stinks, the more bugs come."

Nate nudges the mushroom with the side of his shoe. The flies form a perfect V shape and dive bomb his foot. "Huh?" Nate bumps the stalk again. The flies swoop into a straight line and pelt his leg. "Are you seeing this? It's like they've got a bug commander synchronizing their flights."

"Hive mind," I murmur and kneel for a closer look. The flies are dusty with a thin layer of white powder. "They're all covered in spores."

Nate's eyes meet mine. "More zombie-maker fungus?"

"It's definitely suspicious." I reach into my backpack and pull out an empty sandwich bag. When the wasp buzzes away, I reach for the mushroom using the bag as a glove. But the flies rocket toward my face like spitballs shot from a straw. I cringe and swat them away.

"Lemme handle this. I got a way with bugs." Nate grabs the bag and then ninja kicks the mushroom. It falls over like a freshly cut tree. The flies fan out and Nate swoops in. "Told ya. No sweat."

Nate's methods don't seem quite scientific, but the mushroom's in one piece so I can't complain. He opens a pocket on his cargo shorts and tucks the bag inside. "So, what's next?"

A low buzz hums in the distance and a dark swarm emerges from the shrubs. Wasps. Dozens and dozens of wasps. Bobbing and weaving through the air and heading straight for us.

"We gotta go!" I shout and we race toward the bikes.

We pedal hard, but the swarm follows. I've been around enough bees and wasps to know they don't usually attack unless their hive is messed with. Either these guys are crankier than average or it's got something to do with that fungus. The buzzing grows louder as the wasps get closer. A wing twitches against my ear and something rustles in my hair. I rip out my ponytail holder and slingshot it down the road. A wasp zooms after it.

Nate smacks his knee. "We're under attack!"

I pump my legs with all my might. The dark cloud of wasps thins out. We peel around another corner, until bit by bit, the droning grows fainter, then disappears altogether. My legs are weak and my skin crawls. We skid to a stop.

"I can't go on," Nate pants. "I'm pretty sure gallons of wasp venom are seeping into my veins."

"You got stung?"

"A bunch." Nate rubs a pink, puffy spot on his elbow. "Didn't you?"

I pat down my legs and arms. "I don't think so."

"Lucky." Nate's chin is red and splotchy where another wasp got him.

I reach into my backpack and pull out a pack of alcohol wipes. I hand them to Nate. "I think it was more than luck. You had the mushroom in your pocket. That's what they wanted."

"At least I'm not going into anna-flap-tic shock." Nate sighs and rubs a wipe over his leg. "But I'd kill for an ice pack and a can of pop right about now."

I smile and look to a bend in the road just past a cluster of scraggly bald cypress trees. "There's a vending machine at the bait shop. Think you can make it there?"

Nate groans but starts pedaling anyway. In a few minutes, we're gliding toward The Wormery. We park in front of the shop and I reach into my pocket and dig out some coins. "You want root beer or orange?" I ask, dropping the quarters in and stepping around a sticky puddle at the base of the machine.

"I think we hit the motherlode!" Nate exclaims.

"Don't get too excited," I say, noticing a bunch of red lights. "They're out of everything except diet and some pricey cans of Vitaccino."

"I'm not talking about the pop. You gotta check this out."

I turn. Nate's down on his knees poking a stick at a foot-long crack in the dirt. Fuzzy green carpet grows along the opening. It reminds me of the stuff that turns up on forgotten fridge leftovers. Only this gunk glows.

"The bait shop's covered in nuclear barf and I didn't even bring my video camera."

"It isn't barf," I say, though to be honest, I can't rule that out. It smells like rotten apples and resembles hairy Jell-O. "I think it's more funky fungus."

"Tell me you're not gonna make me add the neon puke to my pocket."

I bite my lip. Nate's shorts are getting a little too full of grossness. "Why don't we just scoop some up and ask Mac about it and the stinky rocket? He knows tons about nature, plus he's got a microscope in the back if we need it."

"I'm down with any plan that doesn't involve me wearing that goo."

I fetch another bag and turn it inside out, using the plastic as a makeshift glove. I scoop up a glob. But as soon as I do, the broken-off piece quits glowing. "Weird," I mumble and seal the top of the bag.

We push into The Wormery, and Bubba Bass, the battery-operated fish mounted on the wall, flips its tail back and forth. The place smells like leather and lazy Saturdays on the lake. Mac hits a button on the register and hands a man in fishing waders his change. "Good luck on the water, Jimbo." Mac waves and the man heads for the door.

"How are you two doing this morning?" Mac calls. He's

got deep brown skin and eyes that crinkle up when he smiles. As usual, he's wearing a ball cap with fishing lures stuck in the sides and a pair of faded overalls. "You got another load of worms for me?"

"Not today," I say, coming to the counter. "But I was wondering if we might be able to use your microscope."

"My scope is your scope." Mac swings open the half-door that separates the front of the shop from the back. He leads us to the workroom where two long wooden tables are pushed against the walls. One's strewn with tackle boxes, fishing hooks, and bobbers. The other has a stack of nature guidebooks, a bug board, and a microscope. "Let me know if you kiddos need anything," Mac calls over his shoulder as he heads back to the register. "And help yourselves to a cold drink. The machine out front's been giving me fits all week."

"You're a good man, Mac." Nate makes a mad dash to the mini-fridge, yanking out two bottles of root beer. He sticks one against the sting on his knee and starts guzzling the other.

I get settled at the table and position the stinky mushroom under the scope. Up close, the strand is mostly smooth with only a few grooves here and there.

"Whatcha seeing?" Nate asks. "Evidence of a hostile takeover?"

I increase the magnification to get an extreme close-up

of the underside of the mushroom. There's a familiar swirly jellyfish shape. It looks a whole lot like the close-up of Ophiocordyceps I saw last night. I pull out Dad's journal and examine the sketch. "There's definitely some similarities."

Mac shuffles into the backroom. "How are things coming in here? Anything I can help with?"

"Just looking at some fungus," I say, shifting my body to block Mac's view of the samples.

"Oh really? Mind if I take a gander?"

My fingers twitch against the base of the scope. I thought I wanted Mac's take on the fungus, but now I'm not sure I'm ready to share this discovery. Then again, this is Mac's microscope. In his shop. I scoot back and show him the rocket-shaped mushroom on the tray and the green fuzz in the bag.

Mac leans over the specimens. "Will you lookie there. I recognize these."

"You do?"

"Dog vomit slime mold and a stinkhorn."

Nate busts out laughing. "You're hilarious, Mac."

Mac grins. "Thank you, Nate. But I'm not joking."

I wrinkle my nose. "Dog vomit? Stink-what?"

Mac points to the bags. "It looks like dog vomit slime mold to me. Only that stuff is usually yellow, not green. Anyway, it's a goofy name but the stuff's not too uncommon after a rain."

"Does it normally glow?" Nate asks.

Mac rubs his chin. "Glow? No, I can't say that it does."

"Well, you might want to check out front," I say. "You've got a patch of something weird growing there."

"I surely will."

I hold up the other bag. "Have you ever known flies or wasps to get aggressive about protecting a stinkhorn?"

Mac's brow wrinkles. "You two are just filled with strange questions, aren't ya? No, I don't reckon I know anything about that, either. Just that the things smell like something died."

"Hmm, interesting," I say, jotting down a note in my journal.

Unusual Traits Observed in Local Fungi

Dog vomit slime mold shows signs of
    bioluminescence

Stinkhorn mushroom increases insect aggression

Hypothesis: Mutant Ophiocordyceps infects not
    just animals, but other species of fungi?

Bubba Bass starts singing back in the shop and Mac glances over his shoulder. "Sounds like I got another customer."

"Well, we should probably get going anyway," I say. "Thanks for letting us borrow your scope."

"Any time." Mac stands and dusts his hands on his overalls. "You know, if you want, I could hang on to those samples and try to do a little digging. I've got a few more guidebooks at home. I could flip through them and see if I can't find something about angry bugs or glowing colors."

"Oh." I'm not sure we should be giving away our evidence. I look to Nate. He shrugs.

I put the specimen back in the bag and lift my hand off the tray. Mac's a smart guy and might be able to offer some more clues. Plus, if Gramma finds the stuff she'll trash it for sure. "Let me know what you figure out, okay?"

"You know it."

Hot, muggy air wraps around us as we wave goodbye and hop on our bikes. "What's next?" Nate asks, scratching at another one of his stings. "You ready to go public with this stuff? We could post all the updates on *The Conspiracy Squad's* channel. Give it a cool title and everything."

"We don't have near enough proof. We can't go shouting from the rooftops that some mutant zombie fungus is taking over the town. I need the Vitaccino board to think I'm smart. Then they'll remember that Dad is smart too and give him his job back."

"But what about after that? We finally stumbled onto something juicy. We gotta seize the opportunity."

"You'll have your moment of glory. Don't worry."

CHAPTER SIXTEEN

Things aren't coming together as quickly as I hoped. I've spent the last week doing tons of research—reading loads and investigating around town with Nate. We found a couple more stinkhorns and a gang of suspicious orb-weavers stretched across the monkey bars at the school playground. I considered bringing one home but figured Gramma would just toss it out too. I settled for a snapshot instead. Now my walls are plastered with sketches of mushrooms and my journal is full of all sorts of random notes.

Unpleasant Facts About Fungi

There's more than a thousand different kinds
   of parasitic fungi.

Every year, tons of people and animals get sick
   from fungus.

Scientists haven't discovered a cure for most
   fungal infections.

I roll to my stomach and smoosh my face into my pillow. What I need is a breakthrough. Ezra's cough isn't getting any better, and he's still running his humidifier day and night. It's like he's trying to turn his room into a South American jungle. The first step in the scientific process is observation. But Ezra's been working so much lately, I've hardly seen him. I sit up and push my hair out of my face, a fresh thought zinging through my head. What kind of scientist lies around waiting for her research subject to come to her?

I leap off the bed and slide my feet into flip-flops. Half an hour later, Nate and I are zooming down the back roads. We pass over the railroad tracks and my gaze trails to Old Man Bell's woods. Deep green boughs stretch over shadowy paths. I wonder whether the fungus still lights up in the dark. Or if the white cloud storms through the trees when no one's looking.

The afternoon sun's beating down on my back when we wheel up to the side of the Vitaccino plant. Half the town works at the factory and the lot is loaded with cars. I scan the fields out back. Workers in sun hats and overalls move through rows of bushes picking berries. But there's no sign of Ezra.

I turn to Nate. "Let's snoop around the fields. See if we can get eyes on Ezra. Try to act natural."

"You got it," Nate says, eyes narrowing to slits, shoulders hunching, and head darting side to side.

I sigh. Nate can't resist hamming it up.

Around back, rows of shrubs are freckled with blueberries and farmhands shuffle about carrying baskets and plucking berries. Sweat rolls down my neck as we slink by, keeping our heads low and avoiding eye contact.

After skulking around the fields for a solid twenty minutes, we've had zero luck. Nate plops down in front of a bush and pops a berry in his mouth. His cheeks are red and his curls are extra poofy from the humidity. "Not to be a Negative Nelly, but it's not looking like Ezra's here."

I push a few damp hairs off my forehead and scan the fields again. Knowing Ezra, he's probably out skateboarding or vandalizing or loafing around somewhere. Maybe he never got a job here at all. He could've made the whole thing up just to score points with Gramma and get under my skin. This entire sticky hot excursion was a waste of time.

We slink back to the front of the plant and grab our bikes. "Wanna pick up a bag of Zesty Onion O's and a Big Guzzle root beer on our way home? My treat," Nate offers.

"Tempting." I tuck a tangle of damp hair behind one ear, trying to remind myself that even big shots like Louis Pasteur and Jane Goodall dealt with disappointment in the field.

Just then, Ezra, Jack, and Zion mosey around the side of the building carrying dusty silver buckets. Before I can duck behind a bush, Ezra's eyes hit mine.

"Mags? Nate?" Ezra frowns. "What are you doing here?"

My gaze darts to Nate, but he's twiddling his fingers and staring up at the clouds. It's his standard innocent bystander pose.

I clear my throat. "It's not a crime to go for a bike ride. Besides, aren't you supposed to be working, not goofing off in the parking lot?"

Ezra gives his pail a shake. "I *am* working. Just got back from grabbing some pop for the crew."

I eye their dusty, empty buckets. The whole story reeks. "Where are the drinks? Why are your buckets all dirty?"

"We just delivered them." Ezra arches a brow. "And the buckets are dirty 'cause this is a farm. Guess you don't know everything after all."

Jack snickers and Zion's eyes drop to his own dingy bucket.

Heat creeps up my cheeks and I squeeze my bike's handlebars. "If you'll excuse us, we've got important business to attend to elsewhere."

"Last time you two had important business, somebody ended up dead," Jack chimes in with a smirk.

"Not cool," Nate mutters, his jaw tensing.

"Lay off, man," Ezra says, eyes on me.

Jack shrugs a shoulder and looks away. "I'd better get back. I'll catch you later."

"Me too." Zion gives an apologetic smile, then shuffles along after Jack.

I push my bike toward the parking lot, but Ezra raises a hand. "Hold up a sec, okay?" He glances over his shoulder and waits until the guys make their way back to the fields. When he speaks again his voice is barely above a whisper. "I need to tell you guys something. You know that fungus you've been freaking out about? You might not be so crazy after all."

I search his face for signs that he's messing with us, but there's no trace of a smile. "Really?"

"The last few days, we've been running errands for the farmhands. On the way, I've sorta popped by Old Man Bell's place."

"Ezra! What were you thinking?"

"You're a brave soul," Nate mutters, looking in awe of Ezra all over again.

"I know I should've stayed away, but I couldn't." He swallows. "I've seen things out there. Weird things."

Nate bobs his head. "I'm digging the sound of this."

I give an impatient toss of my head. "Don't encourage him, Nate."

A full-body cough rolls over Ezra. When he finally

quits, his eyes are watery and bloodshot. "Promise you won't say anything to Gramma. Not until I know more."

I chew my lip. Ezra is looking pastier all the time, like he's been stuck indoors the whole summer even though he's been out in the fields every day. But those woods are the key to understanding what's happening around town. And if Ezra's got inside information, he might be our best shot for solving this mystery. "I'll stay quiet for now, but if that cough gets any worse, we have to tell her."

He nods, then glances over his shoulder.

His right eye twitches and I suddenly get the feeling I'm not going to like what he has to say.

"There's somebody new working out in the woods. He calls himself the caretaker. He's not a normal man. He talks to bugs and trees . . . and they listen."

CHAPTER SEVENTEEN

I f Ezra wasn't so stone-faced, I'd be sure he was joking. "What do you mean they listen?"

"I don't have any proof, but it's like he waves his hands and stuff happens. Branches rattle and bugs swarm his way."

Nate rubs his chin. "As far as you can tell, does this caretaker have any visible robot parts? 'Cause I think I might have a *Midnight Kingdom* issue that explains—"

"Not now, Nate." I shake my head.

Ezra peers at us, his eyes rimmed in pink. "I know I sound nuts, but there's something strange about him. About the whole place."

Ezra does sound a tad bonkers. But there might be something to it. If what he says is even half true, this is gonna require some serious sleuthing. And I'm not sure I can leave it all up to him, no matter how badly I want to avoid a repeat trip to Bell's.

"Listen, I gotta get back before they start asking about

me," Ezra says. "But you guys be careful out there, okay?"

I nod. "You too."

When we get home, Nate gets called in for babysitting duty straightaway and I'm left to ponder on my own who the caretaker might be.

I search for any scientific articles on people commanding plants or bugs but, not surprisingly, can't find a thing. Instead, I write everything Ezra said in Dad's journal. When I finish, I sketch an outline of a shadowy man lurking in the woods. And suddenly I remember that the doberman with the stalk wasn't the only weird photo in my last batch. I fish out the picture I chalked up to the lens being dirty. Sure enough, the blur in the background still looks a whole lot like a person. But the image is too fuzzy to really prove anything.

There's a knock on my door and I tuck the photo under my pillow. Gramma pokes her head in and eyes the journal and pens spread over my bed. "I see you're back at it again. You're so much like your daddy. Always thinking."

I give her a weak grin and shut the journal. "Just finishing up a few things."

She nods. "If you have time for a break, you've got some mail. Must be your lucky day. Two pieces. One of 'em from your daddy."

I spring out of bed and nearly crash into Gramma. She hands me a small cardboard box covered in duct tape and postage stamps. I can already tell this is the one from Dad. In the other hand she's got a creamy envelope. Gramma eyes the letter with pinched lips. "That one's from Lydia Croft. Miss High and Mighty herself. I suppose it's got something to do with that contest you entered."

"The Merit Award!" With all the research I've been doing the last week, the contest had sorta slipped to the back of my mind.

"It sure is nice to see that smile of yours again." Gramma pauses in the doorway. "Well, I'll leave you to your mail."

I run my fingers over the letter and then the box. The handwriting on the one from Lydia is so perfect, it almost looks like it was written by a machine. I flip it over in my hands. It could be a rejection letter telling me my pictures were taken illegally and that I'm not fit to be a naturalist, junior or otherwise.

I set the envelope on my pillow and snag a pair of scissors out of my desk drawer. It takes another minute to cut through the thick layers of tape around Dad's box. When I finally get the cardboard flaps up, I sniff, half expecting the box to smell like an out-of-control campfire, but instead the scent of pine needles fills my lungs. I reach my hand in and pull out a long strand of stones and glass.

Prisms of color glint off it. The top piece is a blown-glass butterfly with a gold and black center and delicate black wings. No, not a butterfly . . . a moth. I smile. It's the *Hemaris diffinis* I told Dad about in my last e-mail.

Small circles of forest-green glass clink against the moth. Below that, two rocks are connected by a thin metal chain—a powder-blue crystal with rough edges and a porous, earth-colored stone.

I hold it all up to the window and watch it glisten. It's by far the most beautiful thing I own. The most beautiful thing that anyone, anywhere could ever own.

I set it carefully on my nightstand and wonder how Dad managed to make this out of all the chaos around his campfire. But that's like him. Always pulling out a surprise when I least expect it.

I reach for a card taped to one of the inside flaps.

Hi Maggie,

I hope you like your sun catcher. The green glass turned out a bit darker than I planned, but I still think it's pretty.

The moth is for my little entomologist in the making. The rocks have a bit of a story too. Remember that hike we took to Sweetwater Basin a few years back? The blue topaz is one of the pieces we picked up in the dry creek. And I found the basalt a couple of weeks ago near my cabin.

Anyway, happy belated birthday, Magnadoodle. I know we're far away now, but in the grand scheme

of things, we're only a couple of stones apart.
Love,
Dad

I press the notecard to my chest. If I squeeze it hard enough, maybe Dad will step right out of the paper and squeeze me back.

It's time we were all together again. And if the letter from Lydia says what I hope it will, it won't be long. I tear into the thick envelope.

Dear Miss Stone,
The Vitaccino Board of Directors is pleased to announce you have been selected as a finalist for its Junior Naturalist Merit Award. The board was intrigued by your discovery of bioluminescent mushrooms in the area. We'd like to learn more about the fungus and your work as an aspiring naturalist. While this is sooner than we anticipated reaching out to candidates, we were so captivated by your entry that we couldn't wait any longer.

We cordially invite you to make a brief presentation regarding your findings at 2 p.m. June 25, at 3113 Emerald Ridge.

Warm Regards,
Lydia Croft, PhD

President of the Greater Thurston County Naturalist
   Society
CEO and Chairman of the Board, Vitaccino
   Health Drinks, Inc.

I've done it. I've really and truly done it! I dance around the room, squealing and jumping up and down.

When I finally quit celebrating, I look back at the letter. June 25 is only three days away. That doesn't give me much time to pull my research together and present a solid case. But it'll have to do.

If all goes well, Dad could be getting his job back in seventy-two hours.

CHAPTER EIGHTEEN

Nate sinks into one of the tree house's beanbag chairs. "I'm pretty sure my ears are gonna bleed if you practice that speech one more time."

My meeting with the board is less than an hour away, and my stomach feels like a bottle of shook-up Coke with a pack of Pop Rocks tossed in for good measure.

"You've got it down, Mags. No worries," Ezra adds, but his back is to me, eyes fixed on something outside the clubhouse window.

I run one hand over my white button-down shirt and navy skirt. "Do I look scientific enough?"

Nate squirts a cloud of cheese spray into his mouth. "You look like you're selling something. I'm telling you, you need to go flashy. Make an entrance."

"For the last time, I'm not wearing your Darth Vader mask."

"Darth Vader was a scientific wonder. Have you ever

thought about the amount of tech that went into keeping Anakin alive?"

"Can we focus on the presentation?"

"You're gonna tell them that something super fungalicious is going down in Shady Pines. You'll show them your photos. Wham, bam, you get the award and they rehire your dad. Simple as that."

"But what if they ask me a question I don't know how to answer? Lydia Croft is a big-time scientist. She knows loads about botany and zoology and all sorts of stuff."

Nate picks up a *Midnight Kingdom* comic and flips through the pages. "You're Magnolia Jane Stone, science nerd extraordinaire. You're gonna do awesome."

"Just makes sure you leave me out of it, all right?" Ezra says, sounding more like his grumpy old self than he has in days.

Nate and I exchange a look. "But earlier you said I could tell them about your cough."

"I changed my mind." Without another word, Ezra turns and swoops down the rope ladder.

"His mood swings are really getting old," I mumble.

"Maybe it's got something to do with the load of zombie-maker spores he inhaled?"

I wipe my palms on the front of my skirt. "He's just being a jerk. It's not the fungus."

• • •

Heat rises in swirls off the asphalt in front of the Marble Falls community. On the other side of the wrought iron gates, a fountain sprays water onto a shining pond. The security guard buzzes me in, and I rehearse my speech as I hurry down the azalea-lined sidewalks. When I reach the Croft's mansion, I ring the bell and a woman in a pressed gray dress opens the door. Her eyes burrow into me.

"Hi. I'm Magnolia Stone. I'm here for a meeting with the board of directors."

"Come along." She leads me past a foyer filled with white orchids in porcelain vases. The sound of voices and tinkling cups drifts from a room down the hall.

Sitting in a circle of plush armchairs are Shady Pines's richest, smartest, and most noteworthy citizens: Mayor Quimble, Dr. Rose Balantino, Superintendent Alistair Silverton, and Charles and Lydia Croft. A silver tray with flaky pastries rests in front of them on the coffee table.

"Hello, Magnolia, so glad you could make it," Lydia says. Her silver hair is shiny and snipped into an angular bob. She wears a crimson pantsuit that reminds me of Amazonian poison dart frogs. "You're Thomas Stone's daughter? He worked for my company recently, I believe."

Heat creeps to my cheeks. I was hoping to save talking about Dad until I'd impressed everyone with my findings. "Yes, ma'am. He works in Yellowstone National Park now.

He's been doing some research on the thermal pools there. It's pretty impressive stuff."

"He always was drawn to pools of liquid." Mayor Quimble chuckles.

A panicky feeling flutters in my stomach. "He didn't mean to let those rats get in the Vitaccino supply. I know he feels really bad about—"

"Don't tease the child." Lydia's eyes snap to the mayor, who wilts like a forgotten houseplant. "Please, Magnolia, proceed with your presentation. We were all quite taken with your photographs."

I glance around the room. Five pairs of eyes stare back at me. I can do this. I've done my research; I know the facts. I open Dad's journal and spread my photos over the coffee table. "You've all seen the pictures of the bioluminescent fungi. But since then, I've made some even more startling discoveries. Insects and mammals around Shady Pines are sprouting unusual growths."

Lydia crosses one deep red pant leg over the other. "What sort of growths?"

"Stalks, like this." I point to the photo of Old Man Bell's doberman.

"And this is what the stalk looks like under a microscope." I motion to the sketch I made of the jellyfish-like tissue.

"Hmm, that's really something, isn't it?" Superintendent

Silverton murmurs, tugging on the edge of his mustache.

Lydia takes a sip of water and lifts her eyes to me. "What do you make of it? Any theories?"

I have to get this part right. Show them that I've got a good head on my shoulders. "I think it may be a type of parasitic fungus called Ophiocordyceps. It attacks carpenter ants in the Amazon rain forest and makes them infect their own colonies. It's also known as the zombie ant fungus." I dart my eyes around the room, hoping I haven't said too much, but they're all leaning forward, gazes fixed on me. "I'm worried it could even spread to . . . people."

"That's quite a theory." Mayor Quimble lifts a gooey pastry from the platter.

Lydia smiles. "I'm sure your father is quite impressed with your discoveries."

"I haven't actually told him much yet. He's been kinda busy with his new job. Plus, I wanted to go about everything the right way. Observe, gather evidence, test my hypothesis and all that."

"Well, you've certainly come to the right group." Lydia leans over the photograph of the doberman. "We'd be happy to assist you in testing your hypothesis, if you'd like."

"Really? That'd be great!" Getting the Crofts on board might be easier than I hoped. "What did you have in mind?"

Lydia taps a manicured finger on her chin. "For starters,

you'd need to gather more evidence. Take additional pictures and find some specimens, too."

All of that would involve returning to Old Man Bell's woods. I've known I needed to go back ever since Ezra told me about the creepy caretaker, but I'd sorta been using my research as an excuse to stall. "I guess I could do that."

"You've truly impressed us, Magnolia. Not many children, or adults for that matter, could have pieced together everything you've brought us." Lydia reaches for a cream-colored envelope on an end table. When she lifts it, I see it has my name written on it in swooping calligraphy. "We don't normally decide this early, but we've all agreed that you have real potential. That's why we're awarding you with Vitaccino's Junior Naturalist Merit Award right now." Lydia extends her hand to me.

"You're giving me the prize?"

"Our hope is that the award money might make it easier for you to continue your research. Buy yourself some shovels and petri dishes. Collect samples. Really dig in and find out everything you can."

I was worried that the board might think badly of me for trespassing to get these pictures, but they haven't even asked where exactly I got them. Instead, Lydia seems eager to keep the investigation going. I wonder if she'd feel that way if she knew all the details. "So you don't think Ophiocordyceps is a danger to anyone? Because I sorta know someone who crossed paths with it and I'm a little worried that—"

Lydia shakes her head. "For a fungus to go from infecting insects to humans would be quite a mutation. I think you're perfectly safe to keep researching. I know you're going to make us all very proud."

Quitting midway through is no way to score points with the board. "I'll do my best."

"Glad to hear it." Lydia presses the envelope into my hand. There's a business card paper-clipped to the back. "I can't wait to hear what you discover."

I take the envelope, then glance at Dad's journal resting on the coffee table. "There was one more thing I was hoping to talk to you about."

"What is it, dear?"

"It's about my dad. Tommy Stone. Like you said, he worked for you. I know things didn't end all that well."

"It was months ago. I've nearly forgotten what all the fuss was about." Lydia smiles.

I don't really believe she's forgotten about the rats swimming in vats of her health drink, but it's nice of her to say it. "That's good, because it's been hard for him to find work close to home, and I'd been thinking, maybe you could give him another chance at Vitaccino."

"I see," Lydia says. "And what was your father's specialty again?"

"He's good with tons of things." I lift the journal off the table and flip through his drawings. "Rocks, plants, astronomy. He's got all sorts of ideas."

"Is that your father's notebook?" Dr. Balantino asks.

"Yes, ma'am." I press the journal close. "I know he could do a lot for your company if he just had another shot."

"I'd be willing to take a look at his research," Lydia says. "Perhaps there's a position with us that might fit his skill set."

I clasp my hands together. "That's fantastic!"

Lydia extends a hand toward the journal.

"Oh." She wants Dad's book. The thought of parting with it feels like giving up my right eyeball. I grip it a little tighter.

"Unless you know a better way for us to see what your father has to offer, without getting his hopes up. Besides, from the sound of it, he's overqualified to be a lab assistant."

"You really think so?"

"No way of knowing for sure yet, but I'm optimistic." Her gaze shifts to the journal. "I'd only keep it for a few days, but if you're not comfortable with the arrangement, I understand."

If I say no now I've got a feeling Vitaccino will never rehire Dad. "My notes are in the back half, but you can tell the difference. My section's labeled 'Maggie's Work.'"

"That will be an interesting read as well." Lydia's fingers close around the journal. "Mind if we hold on to the pictures? There are a few more board members who weren't able to attend today."

"That'd be okay, I guess."

Lydia straightens and points to the section in the journal with the torn-out pages. "It appears something's missing."

I grit my teeth, angry at Ezra all over again. "I lost them. I'm sorry."

She nods. "Well, if they turn up, let us know. The more we can understand about your father's ideas, the better."

The board murmurs, flipping through the photos. Everyone seems to have forgotten I'm here. I shuffle my shoes against a red floral rug. "Dad really is a genius."

Lydia glances up. "And the apple doesn't fall far from the tree. We'll be keeping our eye on you, Magnolia Stone." Lydia flashes a toothpaste-commercial smile, and then returns to studying the journal.

I see myself out.

CHAPTER NINETEEN

As I hustle past a trellis of flashy red roses, I peek into the envelope. There're five crisp one-hundred-dollar bills inside. It's more money than I've ever seen in my life. Not only that, but the board is seriously considering rehiring Dad. Everything I've worked for is coming together. The final piece is solving the mystery at Old Man Bell's. I kick a pebble down the sidewalk and watch it skitter away. It's the last place on earth I want to go, but there's no way around it. It's time I figure out what's really happening there and what it means for Ezra and the town.

At the Marble Falls security booth, Nate's chatting it up with the guard. When he sees me, he heads my way. "How'd it go?"

I hold out the envelope. "I got first prize. And they said they'd consider rehiring Dad."

"Score!" Nate holds up his palm for a high five, and I

give it a slap. "What do you say we hit up Slippery Joe's Water Park? Do the slides till we're so dizzy we barf?"

"Actually, I had another idea." I arch an eyebrow and try to make my voice sound all mysterious and dramatic. "You want excitement, maybe a whiff of danger?"

"Uh, yeah. Have you met me?"

"How do you feel about joining me for a little recon work at Old Man Bell's woods tomorrow afternoon?"

Nate wrinkles his nose. "I thought we decided that place was quarantined. The whole mutant fungi and creepy caretaker thing?"

"You said you wanted excitement."

"Excitement, not death."

"Come on, Nate. I need more specimens. Plus, I've got a plan to make it completely safe."

At dinner that night, I share the news that I've won the Merit Award, but leave out the part about needing to snoop around Bell's place again.

"I'd say this calls for rocky road ice cream," Gramma declares, and heads for the freezer.

I give Ezra's leg a little kick under the table.

"What was that for?" he grumbles.

I hold one finger over my lips and look to the kitchen. Gramma's just getting started filling the first bowl.

"Me and Nate are going back to Bell's tomorrow," I whisper. "We could use your help."

Ezra shrugs one shoulder. "I'm kinda busy. I have a job, you know."

"This is important. We need to figure out what's going on out there."

"I don't think you should go," Ezra says, leaning away from the table with his arms crossed.

"I have to." I glance to the kitchen. Gramma's starting the second bowl. "I'm still researching the fungus for the Crofts and I need to get them some samples. Besides, you're not looking so great these days. We need to know what we're dealing with out there." On top of the dark circles under Ezra's eyes, his skin's taken on a shiny look, like a wax-museum version of himself.

"I'm fine. It's just allergies." He rubs the back of his hand across his nose. "You're wasting time going there. The whole thing's pointless." Ezra pushes away from the table just as Gramma arrives carrying the two bowls.

"Where are you going, Ezra? Don't you want some rocky road?"

"No thanks," Ezra says, giving me a final glare. "I'm tired. I'm going to bed."

Gramma slides into the chair next to me and lifts a spoonful of chocolate to her lips. "Early to bed and skipping dessert. Your brother's really growing up." But she doesn't sound so happy about it this time.

I poke my spoon into my ice cream, not feeling hungry anymore either.

That night, I toss and turn and can't fall asleep until well after midnight. When I finally wake up the next day, it's nearly lunch time. After plates of fish sticks and fried okra, Nate and I suit up for our investigation.

"I look ridiculous." Nate frowns at his reflection.

"You look prepared." I adjust the jumbo-size trash sack around my shoulders. The suits looked cooler in my head. But Gramma's rubber dish gloves, trash bags, and duct tape were the best I could do on such short notice. "Try on the bandanna. We need to make sure the head gear is going to work."

Nate pulls his swim goggles on and tugs the bandana over his nose. Even through the foggy plastic lenses I can tell he's giving me the stink eye. "At least ninety percent of being a hero is looking cool while you're doing it. If we show up at Old Man Bell's like this, we're pretty much guaranteed to die in a really humiliating way."

"Quit griping," I say. "These suits are going to keep us from breathing in any gunk."

"Too bad Ezra didn't have one when Bell was hacking spores all over him."

I catch a glimpse of myself in the mirror, my eyes

framed by fuchsia swim goggles. It feels like we're running out of time. Ezra's getting worse. And we don't have any solid answers. We need help. The Crofts have loads of money and connections and would be able to fix this thing in a snap. But first I've gotta convince them that the fungus is actually a threat. I turn to Nate. "You ready?"

Nate adjusts his goggles. "I was born ready. Well, technically, I was born colicky and a little constipated, but—"

"Let's roll."

I glance at Ezra's closed door. I'd sorta hoped he might surprise me and join in last minute. I even set aside a pair of gloves and an extra trash bag for him. But right after lunch he bolted to skateboard with Jack. Nate and I will just have to solve this on our own.

On the way out, we pass Gramma in the front yard. She squints at our trash bag suits as she snips a wilted hydrangea with a pair of clippers. "You kids heading to a costume party?"

"We're doing some field work, Gramma. Our get-up is scientifically imperative."

"Whatever you say, honey. I'm just glad that award seems to have raised your spirits."

We wave goodbye to Gramma and head down the road. At the railroad tracks, an earthy sweet smell drifts off the stagnant pond. We cross into the woods, and a trickle of sweat runs down the back of my shirt.

Up ahead a ray of sunlight glints off something white and shiny in a tree. Bark grows around a metal square the size of my palm. There's writing on it . . . RESPASSERS WILL BE PROSECU . . . I swallow. It's the remnants of a NO TRESPASSING sign.

Nate spots it too. "Did that tree eat a sign?"

"It must have been there a long time and the bark grew over it." I peer into the woods. Bark creeps over the signs on another dozen trees. Fragments of words peek out: WILL BE PROSECUTED . . . and PRIVATE PROPER . . .

I move from tree to tree, feeling like I've somehow gotten sucked into an old *Twilight Zone* episode. All of the NO TRESPASSING signs that were here a couple of weeks ago are now nearly swallowed up by bark.

"A forest can't do its own landscaping, can it?" Nate asks.

"What?"

"It's just that the signs were keeping people out. If the zombie fungus didn't like that, maybe it buddied up with the trees to change things. Make it so people would come strolling in here without thinking twice."

I run my fingers over the edge of a bark-covered sign. In my fungi research, I read about how trees can talk to each other using fungi. The fungi help the trees find better soil and water reserves. As a thank-you, the trees feed the fungi from their roots. But destroying NO TRESPASSING signs is taking their partnership to the next level. "Fungi don't have feelings. They can't actually want things."

"Maybe not feelings exactly. But stuff wants to survive, right? The signs were keeping people out. Scaring off potential victims. Now anybody might waltz through here. That seems like a mega-win for some evil mutant mushrooms. Villains are always willing to do whatever it takes to rule the world."

The forest is too quiet, like the trees are holding their breath waiting for us to speak. "Whatever it takes," I whisper. I've researched enough to know life can be found in some of the most hostile environments on earth. Adapting. Thriving even. Like the microscopic tardigrades in Antarctica that spend their lives frozen solid. Or the eyeless fish of the deep sea that hunt by detecting changes in water pressure. Life makes a way.

As we march along, Nate pans his camcorder over the still woods. Up ahead, brambles twist around something metallic. A layer of thick green moss stretches across a propeller and patches of mushrooms dot the ground. I push away some of the fuzzy overgrowth on the wing. *Geronimo* is painted in blocky orange letters. It's Old Man Bell's crop duster, looking like it's been rotting here a hundred years.

CHAPTER TWENTY

t's only been two weeks since I last saw the thing in the air, but thick roots curl around its tail and tendrils of ivy carpet the cockpit. Low chirping sounds come from a shadowy opening in a hill behind the plane.

Nate swings his camera toward the crop duster. "And here, ladies and gentlemen, is the ship the extraterrestrials crash-landed in. It may look like your average farm plane, but don't be fooled. This is next-gen alien tech hiding in plain sight."

Nate might be able to laugh it all off, but nothing about this feels funny. I want to collect my samples and get out of here. "Can you get a close-up of the wing?"

"Already on it," Nate says, fiddling with the camcorder's screen.

I'm out of film until I can make it back to Goodman's Pharmacy, so Nate's agreed to document everything, promising to cut his show's audio so the file for the board will be purely scientific footage.

Muggy air rises from the forest floor and my trash bag suit clings to my chest.

As we plunge deeper into the thick overgrowth, we hit the jackpot with all sorts of shining fungi cropping up. "Just a sec. I'm gonna grab a couple." With a gloved hand, I kneel and pluck a speckled toadstool and two chartreuse mushrooms the shape of mini-brains, then seal them in separate plastic bags.

We trudge on, following a worn path that weaves through the trees. But nothing looks familiar anymore. We've definitely gone deeper than on our first visit. Nate stops and tugs my arm. "Check it out." A faded gray cabin with a sagging porch peeks out from the woods. A weathered rocking chair creaks back and forth.

"It must be Old Man Bell's house," I say. A roadrunner weathervane slowly whirrs in the front yard.

"I'm a professional and all, but if something comes climbing out of that ghost hut, I'm probably gonna pee my pants."

"Understood." I swallow a cold lump as we pass the cabin and come to a ridge. A dusky field stretches out beneath us, sheltered from the sun by the forest's thick boughs. Hundreds of gleaming mushrooms of all shapes and sizes pulse, filling the space with eerie color. But they're not scattered randomly over the field in chaotic clusters. Instead, the fungi are lined up neatly like corn or wheat. "How did that happen?" I murmur.

Nate lowers his camcorder, taking it all in with his own eyes. "I don't know, but I don't think I like it."

Something stirs in the underbrush bordering the field. Figures trudge forward in a slow shuffle. Ezra, Jack, and Zion, each carrying a rusty silver bucket.

I smile. Ezra came after all. And he brought backup. But as the three of them slog along, my face slowly falls. Their steps are too in sync. Left, right, left. I've seen that kind of synchronized routine before. The spiders on my window. The bugs on the stinkhorn. And now my brother.

A few more people plod out from the trees, all with buckets hanging on their arms. The group is mostly teenage boys, but I recognize a few grown-ups too. Kirby Filson from the fire department. Taniesha Jones from the deli counter at Lenny's Supermarket. A sudden wind whips through the canopy and every one of them bends down and starts to fill their buckets.

Nate crouches behind a cluster of bushes. "Well, everything here seems perfectly normal and not at all zombirrific. What do you say we call it a day and skedaddle?"

"I told Ezra this place was dangerous. He's not even wearing gloves. He is so busted."

Clouds of white spores rise up around the group, and Ezra's lips look bluer than ever. This is way worse than I imagined. I cup my hands around my mouth and shout, "Ezra!"

His eyes flick to mine and then, like lightning, he drops his bucket and sprints my way. In a few seconds he's climbed the ridge and closed the distance between us. His chest bumps into my shoulder. "I told you not to come." Ezra peers from the mushroom field to the dark forest beyond.

"I have research to do, remember? And unlike you, I'm actually wearing protective gear."

"I'm doing some research too. But you're gonna mess it up," Ezra says, stealing another glance over his shoulder. "The caretaker thinks I work for him, all right? But if he catches you here with your goofy garbage sack shirts, he's gonna know something's up."

Nate rubs his chin. "So you're, like, a double agent, infiltrating the ranks of the fungus underworld?"

"Something like that," Ezra says. "Now get lost before we get caught."

"I'm not going anywhere until you tell me exactly what's happening out here." I plant my feet on the ground.

"Can't you just listen to me for once in our lives?"

"Nope." If Ezra thinks I'm going to fall in line just because he's my big brother, he's got another think coming. Before I can give him a piece of my mind, though, a howl bellows through the treetops; the lights of the mushrooms tremble and then go out completely. Goose bumps skitter down my arms.

"It's back," Nate murmurs.

He's right. Everything feels just like that night when the fungi suddenly went dark.

Ezra's eyes lock on something in the distance. "He's coming."

The wind stirs a few fallen leaves and Nate ducks. "Um . . . who exactly is coming?"

"The caretaker." Ezra stands rigid-straight like a soldier snapping to attention.

"So this is either the moment where the bad guys get locked in an intergalactic dungeon or we suddenly develop superpowers and kick a whole lot of—"

"I don't think either of those is an option right now." I crouch next to Nate.

All the colors of the forest suddenly burst back to life. Nuclear greens and blues blaze so bright I scrunch my eyes shut. It's like a creepy version of the Marble Falls house that always has the gaudiest decorations at Christmas.

"Greetings, visitors," a voice sweeps through the branches. "Welcome to the forest."

CHAPTER TWENTY-ONE

A tall, spindly man in a long dark coat glides between the trees. Something about the length of his nose or the slight stoop in his shoulders makes me think he's old. But then I'm not so sure. His hair is jet-black, and his skin is so smooth it shines like when Gramma slathers on her wrinkle cream at night.

"Who have you brought me today, Ezra?" the man asks, tilting his head.

"This is my little sister, Maggie, and her friend, Nate." Ezra's eyes hover around his boots.

I scowl at Ezra. I don't want this guy knowing my name.

"I am Albert Eldridge, the caretaker of these woods." He extends a hand. "A pleasure to meet you."

Nate lifts his chin slightly. "Hey."

Albert's face and hands have the same faint tint as Ezra's, like after we dye eggs at Easter and the food coloring won't quite wash out. Albert follows my gaze. "The mushrooms discolor the skin. It's of no concern." His hand still sticks out waiting for me to give it a shake.

I cross my arms, and at last Albert slips his hand back into the pocket of his seasonally inappropriate coat.

"How exactly did you end up the new caretaker?" I ask. "Bell just died. Are you related to him or something?"

"Mags, don't," Ezra says in a low voice.

"No relation." Albert's pale irises peer through me. "But I served as his apprentice for many months. It was natural that he leave the property to me."

They haven't even had Old Man Bell's memorial service yet. I don't know a ton about legal stuff, but Albert owning the land seems awfully fast.

Albert lifts a shaggy brow and surveys the field. "Would you like to join the others? There's plenty of work for all."

My heart hiccups and I exchange a quick glance with Nate. "We're not here to join anything. We're just doing some research."

"I see." Albert's face stretches into something resembling a smile. "Please explore wherever you wish."

"Albert's just being generous. You don't really need to hang around," Ezra says.

"They are welcome here."

"Right, of course, sir." Ezra's cheeks flush. "That's very nice of you."

Ezra says he's investigating, but it looks more like he's just here to suck up to Albert Eldridge. If I'm going to gather decent evidence, I need answers. And the new caretaker might be the only one who's got them. "Why do you have my brother picking mushrooms? Why aren't any of the workers wearing gloves? Aren't you worried about their safety?"

A buzz whirrs from a nearby shrub and a lone bumblebee emerges, flying in an erratic zigzag. "You have many questions," Albert says and stretches out a long, knobby finger. The bee lands and perches on the tip.

Nate takes a scrambling step back. "Um sir, there's a bee on your—"

Ezra glares at me. "My sister likes to think she knows a lot about science and stuff. Don't worry about her. She was just about to leave," Ezra says, then drops his voice and says to me, "Just shut up, okay?"

"I do know a lot about science and stuff." My face is hot and I'm pretty sure I'm turning red. Ezra's always treating me like a baby who doesn't know anything. I've been reading about fungi nonstop for days and now that I'm here, I'm not leaving without answers. I spin back to Albert. "Are you aware that invasive mutant mushrooms are likely growing in these woods?"

"Maggie, I'm serious. Be quiet."

"Let her speak." Albert flicks his hand and the bumblebee glides away. "Ezra, you may return to the others."

Behind Albert's back, Ezra mouths something, but I

can't tell what. I shrug and he rolls his eyes, then marches away.

Nate pokes me in the ribs. "Check it out." As Ezra rejoins the group, they all begin to move in a single-file line, bending to pluck mushrooms in perfect time. Up, down. Up, down.

I've seen enough.

"Those workers have spores all over them. Half of them are glowing. You've gotta call them in and spray them down with bleach or something."

"It seems . . . you dislike fungus." Albert pronounces each word slowly.

"Those mushrooms might be infected with mutated Ophiocordyceps, a jungle fungus that attacks—"

"Carpenter ants in South America." Albert bends and plucks a glimmering toadstool. He tucks the tiny umbrella-shaped fungus behind one ear. "Yes."

I blink. "You're not worried about infection?"

Albert tilts his chin. "There's nothing to fear. Ophiocordyceps is our friend." He pulls the umbrella from his ear and pops it in his mouth.

I shriek, "Don't eat that!" Nate gags.

He chews, then swallows. A green shimmer runs down his neck. "Delicious and nutritious."

My jaw drops. "Are you crazy?"

"They're perfectly safe. That's why we harvest them.

Full of vitamins and minerals. Wonderful for the bones and the mind."

"Those mushrooms are bad news. Shady Pines has critters with stalks shooting off their bodies. This is a serious problem," I say.

The workers snap their heads in my direction. Kirby and Taniesha take a few dragging steps away from the others. Kirby stretches out one arm, looking so much like a classic zombie that I'd crack up if he weren't stomping my way.

"I don't think we wanna tick off the horde," Nate whispers.

"Everything is under control." Albert shifts one finger and Kirby and Taniesha rejoin the group. "I think a demonstration is in order."

I really don't want a show-and-tell from Albert. But since he's got such a devoted following, I think we'd better hear him out.

He snaps his fingers and a skinny boy with pasty skin and dusty yellow hair shuffles our way. He carries one of the ever-present silver buckets. Albert takes it from him and then waves his hand. The boy trudges back to the others.

I peek over the rim of the bucket. It's filled with a white goo that shines like the fat that hardens in the pan after Gramma fries bacon.

"What is that?" I ask. There's a smell like Elmer's glue mixed with pond water.

Albert dips his finger into the bucket. "A remedy for your troubles."

Nate scrunches his nose. "Uh, could you be a little more specific?"

"Observe." Albert kneels and spreads a small glob on a patch of shimmering fungi. It sizzles and froths until a white foam forms. When the bubbles die down, all that's left is a burnt brown patch.

"Whoa," Nate says. "It roasted it from the inside out."

Albert gazes down at the shriveled mushrooms with a pensive look. "It would appear that way."

Nate and I trade glances. There's something seriously off about the new caretaker.

Albert stretches out his hand. The finger that he dipped into the bucket is not only completely burn-free, but it's also no longer blue. "Spread it on any fungi that worries you. It will alleviate all your concern."

Nate cocks his head to one side. "But what about—"

I clear my throat. "This seems like it'll do the trick. Thanks."

"You are welcome." Albert's pale eyes hover over me.

I dart my gaze away. "Well, I guess that's everything, then."

"Don't forget the remedy." Albert hands me the jelly-filled bucket.

"Right." The gel quivers in the pail.

"Do come back and visit us again soon." At that, he turns and slinks through the clearing toward the workers.

I reach for Nate's arm and we hurry through the woods without saying another word. When we make it to the downed crop duster, Nate steals a glance at me. "So, we really gonna spread this stuff around town?"

I peer down at the shiny white goo. "Not a chance."

CHAPTER TWENTY-TWO

We trot across the railroad tracks, back to our side of Shady Pines. Albert's cure gave me an idea.

"I want to run tests on the fungi. See if we can find our own treatment."

"Shouldn't you leave that to the people in lab coats with little glass beakers?" Nate asks.

"You saw how Ezra was acting. He's bad off and I want answers," I say. "We oughta stop by The Wormery, too, and see if Mac's had any luck with the samples."

"Don't bother. The fam went out for slushies last night and Dad grabbed a tub of bait on the way home. I was supposed to let you know the fungus gunk still has Mac stumped."

"Well then, maybe we could question Jack and Zion," I say as we turn down the gravel road of Raccoon Creek Trailer Park. "Maybe they'd tell us more about Albert Eldridge than Ezra did. We'll need the full scoop before we call in backup."

"But they're all out in the woods having a mushroom party right now, so I'd say that's a no go."

I tap my fingers on my lips. "What if we pay them a surprise visit first thing tomorrow morning?"

"First thing after Bell's memorial, you mean. It's tomorrow, remember?"

"Oh, right," I reply.

"While we were stomping around his place, I kinda wished the old guy might come out shaking his fists at us again. Instead, we got the Spore King and his minions."

"Spore King? That's creepy, Nate."

"Thanks." He grins. "I've been working on it since we hightailed it out of the woods. You gotta admit that dude's got villain written all over him. Did you see his trench coat? That's, like, standard-issue bad guy wardrobe."

A truck engine backfires as Nate's dad pulls into the park. "I gotta go. I told my dad I'd clean my room and now I've got about negative three seconds to do it."

Long shadows fall over the lawn as I tuck Albert's jelly behind the honeysuckle bush and head inside. The house is quiet, and two new messages blink on the answering machine. One from Gramma saying she has to stay late at work. An oil spill with the deep fryer. And another from Ezra saying he's going bowling with Zion and he'll be home late. Considering an hour ago he was tromping through the woods, kissing up to Albert Eldridge, I'm pretty sure that's a big fat lie.

The sooner I can gather conclusive evidence and get some backup, the better.

I warm up Gramma's chicken tetrazzini and think about what we've got around here that I can test on the mushrooms. As I chew a cheesy bite, the kitchen phone rings.

I grab it after the first ring. "Hello?"

"Hey, sweetie, it's me."

"Dad!" I squeal. "You're back at your cabin?"

"For the night I am." Dad sighs. "Summers here are crazy. They've got me running all around the park." I picture Dad's face, his cheeks prickly with stubble, his lips turned up in a sideways smile.

"I got the sun catcher you made. It's so pretty."

"I had fun hunting down the basalt for it. Whenever you kids come up here for a visit we'll have to do a hike and see what other rocks we can find."

I shrug a shoulder. "Yeah, unless you've already moved back here . . . then we might not have time for a visit."

There's a pause, and when Dad speaks again his voice sounds softer, more careful. "I know that's what you're hoping for, Mags, but there just aren't a lot of jobs in Shady Pines."

"Well, I've been working on something new. I didn't want to say anything until I knew more, but I've nearly got it all worked out for Vitaccino to rehire you." My stomach flutters as I race out the words.

Dad clears his throat. "Vitaccino, huh? That's something."

He doesn't sound excited. But bringing Dad home has been my mission since the day he left. The Merit Award, the trip to Old Man Bell's woods, meeting with the board—everything was for him. "Don't you wanna come back?"

"I want to be with you kids. More than anything. I think about you all the time."

I poke my fork into my casserole leftovers. Dad didn't really answer my question. "Lydia Croft said you're over-qualified to be a lab assistant. She thinks she might have something even better for you."

"Hey, kiddo, I know it doesn't always seem like it, but I've got things under control."

He doesn't get it. He's way off in the wilderness of Wyoming. Maybe he's too busy or far away to remember that we're all back here, missing him every day. "It's been six months. That's a really long time."

Dad pulls in a long breath. "This is hard for me, too. Really hard. But I'm working as fast as I can. That's why I go wherever they ask me, take every extra shift. As soon as I get promoted, I'll be stationed someplace permanent, close to the schools. Then you and Ezra will be able to move out here and we'll all be together again."

I blink. Dad expects us to leave Shady Pines? And

Gramma and Nate and everything I've ever known? That's not the plan. Him coming back is the plan. "So you're never moving home?"

"I didn't say that. But . . . I grew up in Shady Pines. It's a small town and there's not a lot of hope for a person to get ahead there, especially in the sciences. I've always dreamed of doing something big, really seeing the world, you know?"

It's just like Ezra said. Dad wanted something more. More than us. More than home. Only I could never see it before. "Lydia Croft is a scientist and she's doing great things here. She lives in a huge house and has tons of money. Maybe it's not Shady Pines that's the problem."

"Maggie, that's not fair."

"Well, neither is leaving us behind to explore a bunch of stupid geysers and rocks. Things keep happening and you're not here for any of it." I spent half the summer figuring out how to help Dad. But it turns out he never wanted that at all. My head throbs. I shove my plate of tetrazzini into the sink. It lands with a crash.

"Magnolia, please. You're not letting me explain."

I grip the edge of the sink and peer down at the sunflower border of my tetrazzini plate. A thin crack runs down the middle. "Then explain."

"Someday soon we're all going to be together again and everything will be better. I promise you."

I think about Old Man Bell hacking out spores and Ezra zombie-walking in the woods. "It might not be soon enough. Ezra's been sick, and there's a weird guy in—"

"Ezra's sick? Has Gramma taken him to the doctor? Because if she's worried about the money, she knows I'll pay for it, whatever it costs."

"It's not exactly the type of sickness Dr. Warbley can help with." I'm not sure I wanna tell Dad all the details. He already thinks Shady Pines is a dump he'd rather leave behind. There's no need to add zombie fungus to the strikes against us.

"Ezra won't take my calls anymore," Dad says. "Or when he does, he barely says a word."

Dad sounds so disappointed that I can't help but feel sorry for him. "Ezra misses you. He's just got a different way of showing it."

"I'm sorry. I've made this rough on everybody."

"It's okay." I don't know what else to say. I hate having Dad so far away. And I'm still mad, but not so mad that I want to end the call in a fight. "Can I ask you a question?"

"Anything."

"Do you know of any household goods that can kill mushrooms?"

Dad chuckles. "You doing a little experiment?"

I twist the phone cord around my hand. "Something like that."

"Check the medicine cabinet. Anything antifungal is worth a shot."

"Thanks," I say.

"I love you, Magnolia."

"You too, Dad."

CHAPTER TWENTY-THREE

rummage up athlete's foot spray and a tube of ring-worm cream. They both say "antifungal" right on the container, so I'm counting that as a win.

I tug on Gramma's dishwashing gloves, grab my supplies, and head behind the trailer. My bagged mushroom samples have all quit glowing, but still look fleshy and alive.

I flip to a fresh sheet on a pad of lined paper—since Lydia borrowed Dad's journal, it'll have to do.

Mushroom Killer Experiment
Specimen One: Squirted down with athlete's
   foot spray
Specimen Two: Spread ringworm cream on with
   a plastic knife
Specimen Three: Poured on a generous dose of
   Albert's jelly
Specimen Four: Control group. It gets nothing.

Back inside, I type some notes for my report, then hit print. Dad made it pretty clear Shady Pines isn't where he wants to be, but I've got to see this thing through. It's my scientific duty.

I glance to the bulletin board hanging above the computer. There's a photo of me and Dad pinned in one corner. He's smiling and his arm's draped over my shoulder. I swallow hard. I know I shouldn't keep hoping. But part of me still thinks there's a chance the Crofts just might offer Dad a job so amazing it'll be impossible for him to say no. Vice president of scientific research. Chief discoverer. Chairman of all things interesting and important. It may be a long shot, but Dad's the one who always says, "You gotta have big dreams to do big things."

The next morning my bedroom door swings open bright and early. Gramma flounces in wearing a coral dress with purple polka dots. "We've got Bell's service, hon. Put on something cheerful."

"Aren't you supposed to wear black?"

"That's what your brother said too." Gramma tsks. "How's anybody supposed to feel better if everybody goes around wearing gloomy sacks?"

I hurry and get dressed—still opting for all black—and grab a blueberry muffin from a platter in the kitchen. I swallow it down in a few big bites, then jog to the front door. "I'll be ready in a sec. I gotta get Nate." Plus, I need to check on my mushroom-killer experiment, but Gramma doesn't need to know that part.

On the way out, I grab my notebook, rubber gloves, and a trash bag, then skitter down the porch steps. My test groups are all still perfectly lined up. The ones I hit with the athlete's foot spray and the ringworm cream are a little soggy but overall about the same. But the last two— the one I gooped up with Albert's cure and the control group—have changed. And not in a good way. Albert's group hit a growth spurt overnight. Three shimmery mushrooms the color of toothpaste sprouted from the pile of white jelly. Two more crept over to the control group.

Albert's jelly doesn't kill mushrooms. It GROWS them.

Mushroom Killer Experiment Results

All tested remedies useless against mutated Ophio.

Albert's cure is bona fide miracle grow for mushrooms.

I tuck my nose into my shirt and scoop all the samples into the trash bag. I haul it up to the tree house and shove everything in a corner. When I finish, I toss the rope ladder up into the clubhouse. Headquarters is officially quarantined.

I hurry to Nate's and ring the bell. He opens the door wearing a pair of faded *Midnight Kingdom* pajamas. I frown. "Bell's memorial, remember?"

"Can't. I'm stuck babysitting the twins."

"What about researching later?"

"My dad will be back in a couple of hours. Just come by after the service." A sippy cup rockets through the air and pelts Nate in the shoulder, splattering grape juice across his neck. "I gotta go."

A car horn blares. "Move your buns, Magnolia. We've got the dearly departed to honor."

The church's wooden pews are shiny and smell like lemon-scented cleaner. Purple-and-blue-tinged light streams in from the stained-glass windows. Besides me, Gramma, and Ezra, only three other people are here: Pastor James behind the pulpit and Sheriff Huxley and Deputy Ronald up in the third row.

"Guess Bell didn't have too many friends," I whisper to Gramma.

"It's not polite to speak ill of the deceased." Gramma fans herself with a leftover bulletin from last Sunday's services. "But of course he didn't have any friends. A person can't go holing themselves up in the woods for eighty years if they want to be popular."

I glance at the lone vase of daisies at the front of the

church. Bell tried to warn us. He knew something dangerous was living on his land. Out of the corner of my eye, I see Ezra slump deeper into the pew. I imagine how things might be different if we'd never gone out exploring that night. If Ezra hadn't tried to save Bell and gotten too close. We wouldn't be sitting here now, that's for sure.

Pastor James glances around at the nearly empty sanctuary. "Well, I suppose we'd better get going." He rests one hand next to a framed photograph of Old Man Bell wearing his wrinkly hat and denim overalls. "We've come here to honor the life of one of our own. He wasn't close with many, but he was a member of our community all the same."

I close my eyes and say a speedy prayer that the service wraps up quick. I need to get back to gathering evidence for the only people in town with the smarts and resources to fix this thing.

After reading from the Psalms and leading us in a round of "Amazing Grace," Pastor James finally closes his hymnal. "Anyone who'd like to say a final goodbye to Hiram Bell is welcome to come up front."

I don't really know how to say goodbye to a photograph so I stay in my seat. The deputy slides out from his aisle and trudges toward the front. He's holding three loops of silver chain. He drapes them over the photo of Bell, then returns to his pew.

"Now, that's a funny thing to do," Gramma murmurs.

"What is it?"

"What sort of person gives dog collars to a dead man?" she says under her breath.

"Dog collars?" I crane my neck. Sure enough, a metal name tag hangs from each of the silver chains. "Why would the deputy give collars to . . . ?"

The snarling dobermans. Their eerie howls as the lights went out in the woods.

The strange stalk growing from one of their lips.

The air in the sanctuary is too thick.

Maybe the dogs got new collars. Maybe they're curled up somewhere right now, gnawing on bones and dreaming of sinking their teeth into trespassers.

Or maybe they aren't.

"You ready to go, Magnolia?" Gramma rises, purse in hand.

"Um . . . can I have a second?"

"All right, hon, but try to make it quick. I've got a broccoli rice casserole to make for LuEllen Marpa. Her kitty bit her finger pretty bad last night and then ran off into the woods after a family of opossums. Poor thing's devastated."

Ezra sits up straighter, suddenly looking a lot less zombified. "I'm gonna hang back a minute too, Gramma."

"That's a good boy." She smiles and saunters down the aisle.

"We need to talk, Mags," Ezra says, fingers twitching.

Before I can answer, the sheriff and deputy pass by and I hop to my feet. "Morning officers, how do you do?"

The sheriff shuffles his cowboy hat from one hand to the other. "Right nice of you kids to come out and pay your respects. I'm sure Bell would think kindly of you for it."

I bite my lip. "I noticed you put dog collars on Bell's picture. And I was just wondering why. I mean, weren't you planning to train them? Did someone adopt the dogs or . . ."

The sheriff dips his head. "I'm sorry to say things didn't work out like we hoped. The dogs got real sick, skin rash, weird things growing out their ears. Took 'em down to Dr. Laghari, but she said she'd never seen anything like it. When they turned on us, that's when we knew something had to be done."

I tug on the hem of my shirt. "What had to be done?"

"We put them down. That's what you gotta do in situations like this, kiddo."

They wave goodbye, and I think I'm going to be sick all over my patent leather shoes. "In situations like this." When something gets sick and changes . . . for the worse.

The dobermans were infected, and now they're dead. I turn to Ezra. Colored light from the sanctuary's stained-glass windows falls over him, tinting his face shades of violet and cobalt. "They died, Ezra. Because of the spores."

"I know," Ezra replies, and for a moment the glazed-over look in his eyes lifts completely. "There's something you need to know. What's happening in the woods. It didn't start with Bell or Albert."

"What do you mean?"

Ezra's hand slides into his pocket and starts to pull something out, then stops midway.

"What is that?" I ask, a sick feeling spinning in my stomach.

"The Crofts." Ezra's jaw tenses, like it's a struggle to get the words out. "They own the land. Old Man Bell worked for them."

"That doesn't make sense." I shake my head. "If the land was the Crofts', then they'd know about the fungi growing there. But neither of them said anything when they saw my photos."

"I told you, I did some investigating of my own. I found stuff." Ezra's hand fidgets at his pocket again.

"Show me."

A bead of sweat rolls down Ezra's temple as he slides out a crumpled photograph. The cloudy look that's become too familiar slowly drifts over his face. He shoves the picture into my hand. "I gotta go." He turns and jogs down the aisle.

I peer at the crinkly photo. It's three people in white lab jackets. Lydia and Charles Croft and a man with jet-black hair and pale blue eyes. Goose bumps prickle along my arms. He's not as pasty in the picture, but it's definitely him. The new caretaker, Albert Eldridge.

CHAPTER TWENTY-FOUR

I race to the car, but when I get there, Gramma's alone.

"Where's Ezra?"

"He saw Jack and Zion skating down to Lil' Saucy's for the lunch buffet and decided to tag along." Gramma studies my face. "You okay? You look mighty flustered."

"We need to follow them and make him come home. He can't leave the house until further notice."

"My, my, someone's getting a bit big for her britches. Why don't you leave the rule-making to me and your daddy?"

"I'm not kidding." It's time she knew what we were really up against. The whole truth. "There's a parasitic fungus living in Bell's woods. It used to just infect ants, but it's mutated or something, and other species are getting sick too. Maybe even people. Like Ezra."

Gramma sighs. "Magnolia Jane, will you listen to yourself? No fungus is taking over this town or your brother. You're upset because Bell passed away."

"This isn't about Bell . . . well, it sorta is, but not the way you think. Please, Gramma. Bell's dogs are dead. LuEllen's cat is probably infected too. This is serious!"

"I want you to take a deep breath and relax. You're starting to turn red in the face from all your hollering."

"It's better than turning blue," I mutter.

"Pardon?"

I shake my head. "Nothing." Gramma's never gonna believe a zombie-maker fungus is on the loose in Shady Pines. If I want help, I'll have to go to the only people with answers.

As soon as we pull into the driveway at home, I jump out of the car and race to Nate's.

"What's set your legs on fire this time, Magnolia Jane?" Gramma whirls her head in my direction.

"Science stuff," I call.

"If it's not one thing it's another," she says, climbing up our porch steps. "I'm heading to LuEllen's in a bit. Buzz me if you need me."

I wave to her and ring Nate's doorbell. Glory, his basset hound, pokes one eye open, then gives a long yawn. As soon as Nate opens the door, I blurt, "There've been more developments in the fungus situation."

He runs a hand through his mess of curls. "What kind of developments?"

"The kind that require an emergency visit to the Croft mansion."

"Are you serious?"

"Deadly. Grab your camcorder and I'll update you on the way."

We're out of breath when the iron gates of Marble Falls glide open. "So you're telling me the Spore King used to work with the Crofts?" Nate stares down at the photo. "And that they own the land at the epicenter of the outbreak?"

"Like I said, they've got some explaining to do."

The housekeeper barely lets us in this time, but when I flash the photo of Albert and the Crofts, she finally agrees. With plenty of huffs and puffs, she escorts us down an unfamiliar corridor to a large office. Lydia sits behind a spotless desk and Charles leans over her shoulder. When the housekeeper clears her throat, they both glance up at us.

"I'm sorry to interrupt, but they insisted on seeing you."

"Not a problem." Lydia waves the housekeeper away and motions for me and Nate to come in. "What a surprise, Magnolia and . . . ?"

"This is Nate Fulton. He's been helping me with some of my research."

"It's nice to meet you, Nate." Lydia gives a tight smile. "But I'm a little surprised to see you back so soon. We've barely had time to look through everything you left us."

"This couldn't wait." I nod to Nate and he raises his camcorder. "We went back to the woods yesterday and got footage of what's happening there. You need to see this."

Lydia and Charles peer down at the small screen on the side of the camera. Nate hits a few buttons and the video starts playing. There's the radiant emerald and aquamarine of the bioluminescent fungi, then the downed crop duster. All of a sudden audio cuts in. "And here, ladies and gentlemen, is the ship the extraterrestrials crash-landed in." Nate fumbles with the player but manages to turn it up louder instead of stopping it. "It may look like your average farm plane, but don't be fooled. This is next-gen alien tech—"

"That wasn't supposed to happen," Nate stammers, jabbing at more buttons.

"I don't understand." Lydia glances from me to Nate. "Is this some kind of joke?"

"He makes funny videos. He was supposed to mute it."

Nate's muttering to himself and flipping through videos on the camera. "Sorry, Mags. I shouldn't have come. Science isn't really my thing." He turns and races down the hall.

"Wait, Nate!" But he's already disappeared around the corner.

Lydia blinks up at me. "Well, that was unexpected."

"The video was a mistake, but something really is going

on out there. The fungus I told you about is spreading fast. Someone has to stop it. I could really use your help."

Lydia folds her hands. "We're trying to help you, Magnolia. We selected you as our Merit Award winner, remember? We're reviewing your father's research. But you have to do your part too."

"I've tried. But the thing is, my brother's been working in those woods and he keeps getting sicker every day. And it's not just him. Old Man Bell's dogs got into the fungus too and now . . . they're dead. Ophiocordyceps is dangerous."

"That does sound worrisome." Lydia's eyes shift to Charles. "But what makes you think we're the right people to offer assistance?"

I swallow and pull the photo from my pocket. "My brother gave this to me. He says you own the land and that Bell worked for you."

The color drains from Lydia's face. "I see."

"I told you we should've handled this differently," Charles mumbles.

Lydia places one hand on Charles's arm. "We would have said something sooner about supporting his farming efforts, but Bell was a very private man. He wouldn't have cared for any publicity."

"What about Albert Eldridge? He's in that photo too. And now he's hanging around the woods, calling himself the new caretaker."

Lydia sighs. "He used to work at our plant, then transferred to the woods about the time your father left our employment. He's recently become something of a problem."

"All the people working in the woods follow him around like he's their master."

"We should've fired him months ago," Charles grumbles.

He's missing the point. "What you need to do is get rid of that fungus."

A vein in Charles's forehead bulges. "You're a little girl. You don't get to tell us what to do."

"There's no need for all that," Lydia says in a too-calm voice, as if we're all just sitting around chatting about what a hot summer it's been.

"Bell is dead. His dogs are dead. Neon mushrooms and zombified bugs are cropping up all around town. You've gotta quarantine those woods and send out a clean-up crew to all the infected sites. And the people, like my brother, they need your help."

Lydia clears her throat. "Those are interesting suggestions. We'll be sure to look into the matter."

"That's it?"

"We're grateful for the information, and we'll take care of things on our end." Lydia folds her hands. "Our number one priority is always doing what's best for the community."

The Crofts aren't jumping to their feet. They're not calling in help. They want me to leave. "That's not good enough."

Charles slams his half-empty glass down on the desk. "My dear girl, it's going to have to be good enough because—"

"Magnolia." Lydia stands and opens a drawer. She pulls out Dad's journal and hands it to me. "We did finish reviewing your father's notebook. You were right. He really is a bright one. We made a mistake letting him slip through our fingers. We're planning to call him later on this afternoon and offer him a supervisor role. Do you think he'd like that? He could start as early as next week."

My heart gallops and I press Dad's journal close. Dad home in a week? All of us together again. We could take a trip to Lake Williams or hike to Sweetwater Basin. Go on road trips and eat picnic dinners on a sea of wildflowers.

Lydia glances at Charles, then smiles. "We'll get everything squared away. You don't need to worry about a thing."

I blink, then realize what's happening. Lydia is bribing me. And deep down, I know Dad doesn't want the job. He wants a life of adventure. And even if he did want to come home, this isn't the right way. The Crofts aren't impressed with Dad or me. The job offer is to make sure I keep my mouth shut.

Lydia and Charles smile again, but this time I'm not buying it. Those aren't nice smiles, they're evil.

I slap on a smile of my own and shove down what I

really want to say. "Have a nice day." I turn for the door.

"One more thing before you go," Charles says, coming around the desk toward me. "If this news were to somehow get out to, say, the sheriff, ask yourself who he'd believe, a kid from Raccoon Creek Trailer Park or the people whose tax dollars pay his salary. We've got every permit and license saying we're not doing a thing wrong. It'd be an open and shut case."

I stand in the center of the room, feeling like a helium balloon that's had all the air sucked out of it. Charles is right. All I've got is a few photos and some wrinkly mushrooms. If I couldn't even convince Gramma that the fungus was dangerous, I don't stand a chance with the sheriff.

"It was lovely seeing you again, Magnolia," Lydia says, her eyes frosty as the icicles growing in the back of Gramma's freezer.

I couldn't make the Crofts help Ezra, Dad won't be coming home, and the fungus will keep right on spreading. I failed. With everything.

I wind down a long, dim corridor, passing a massive portrait hanging on the wall. A man in a safari hat with a monkey perched on one shoulder. These are the kind of people the Crofts are. Larger than life. Winners who get what they want. There's a gold plate underneath the painting: FITZWILLIAM CROFT SR., AMAZON RIVER, SOUTH AMERICA, 1965.

I stick my tongue out at the safari-hat-wearing Croft. His monkey glares back at me with mocking eyes. I find my way to the front door and charge out, nearly crashing into Nate.

"Hey, Mags." He hangs his head. "I don't know what happened with the video. I hope I didn't mess things up too much."

"It wouldn't have made any difference," I say as we walk beneath a pergola wrapped tight with wisteria vines. "They know about the fungus and they aren't going to help. This might sound crazy, but I think they even had me gather samples hoping something bad might happen so that I'd just go away."

Nate raises his brows. "You really think they'd try to take you out like that?"

"I can't prove it, but I wouldn't put anything past them."

Nate pulls two green cans out of the pockets of his cargo shorts. He tosses one to me. "How's this for sticking it to the man? I found a six-pack sitting by the front door, looking all frosty and prime for the guzzling. I kinda already drank the first four, but I saved these two for us." Nate cracks the top of his can and takes a big swig. "Normally I wouldn't pilfer other people's pop, but I had a feeling those guys would turn out to be baddies."

Nate takes another slurp. "This stuff is good. Not five-bucks-a-pop good, but still, pretty dang tasty." He turns the can and reads the side. "With a proprietary blend of all-natural ingredients derived from the Amazon rain forest, Vitaccino eases the mind and heals the body." A drizzle of Day-Glo green fizz hangs from his lip.

Condensation runs down the side of the can and my brain buzzes. Amazon rain forest. Day-Glo green. Old Man Bell's woods.

"Don't drink that!" I whack the can out of his hand. Neon drops splatter across the pavement.

"Sheesh, Mags! What was that for?"

My head whirls as all the pieces finally click together. "Vitaccino's secret ingredient is Ophiocordyceps!"

CHAPTER TWENTY-FIVE

can feel myself zombifying!" Nate cries as he fills his mouth with water from my kitchen faucet.

"No talking. Keep gargling," I say as I click through the Vitaccino website on the desktop computer.

"I don't wanna become one of the Spore King's minions," Nate blubbers through a mouthful of water.

"People have been drinking Vitaccino for years. Half the town would be infected if the stuff was too dangerous."

Nate spits into the sink. "You just told me the secret ingredient was mutant fungus. That can't be good."

"I need you to stay calm and not freak out on me, okay?"

"I can't make any promises. I already got stung by a load of zombie wasps and now this. I'm not sure who's in control of my brain anymore."

I shake my head and click on a video. A man in a flannel shirt walks through a sunny field that looks nothing like Old Man Bell's woods or the Vitaccino farm. He strolls past a red barn with sunflowers swaying in the breeze.

"Vitaccino uses the highest quality ingredients to create the finest products on earth. With a proprietary blend of Texas blueberries, citrus fruits from the groves of Florida, and mycelia from the Amazon rain forest, Vitaccino delivers a powerful punch of nutrients."

"Mycelia? That's the thing that means mushrooms, right?"

I nod.

"Fantastic, even the advertising dude just confirmed I'm gonna die."

I don't like this either, but I can't have Nate losing his mind in my kitchen. "Just settle down. Nobody's dying."

I click on another tab. It's got a chart that lists the ingredients: guava nectar, blueberries, orange juice, lime, and mushroom stems. There's no mention of Ophiocordyceps—that wouldn't be good for business—but if the description is even remotely accurate then maybe we're okay. "It's the spores that are infectious. Vitaccino's made with the stems. I think you might be all right."

"You sure?"

"Lots of rich, fancy people drink the stuff by the case. I doubt the Crofts are trying to kill off their customers. So unless they all of a sudden changed the recipe, you're safe," I say.

"And what would make us think the recipe's changed? It's not like a new caretaker came along and got a bunch of zombified townspeople to scoop mushrooms for him. Oh wait . . . that's exactly what happened!"

"You know, you didn't have to drink quite so many of them."

"What can I say? Pop is my kryptonite. And now it's really gonna be the end of me."

"We're going to figure this out and find a way to stop the Crofts."

"How? We don't have enough proof to pin anything on them. It'd be our word against theirs. We're doomed, Maggie."

"Just let me think for a second." Visions of Nate zoned out and plucking mushrooms in the woods skitter through my head. I need to focus on solutions, but this is way beyond my level of know-how. "We need help."

"From who?"

The first person I think of is Dad. Maybe I'll get lucky and he'll be in an area with coverage. I grab the phone and dial. It goes straight to voice mail. "Dad it's me. It's about Ezra. Remember when I said he was sick? Well, I know what's causing it. There's a fungus growing in Old Man Bell's woods. Anyway, I need you to answer your phone. I know you don't want to come back here, but Shady Pines is in trouble." I pause, shoving down a flood of hot, angry words that want to boil out. Dad should be here right now. He never should have left. "If you could just call me—"

The phone beeps telling me my time's up, and my message is cut off. I slam the phone down. Dad was always our rock. No matter what happened, he was there with a smile or a story about some fascinating, exotic place. And I'd feel better. But now, when I need him most, he's a thousand miles away.

"I'm feeling an urge to start zombie-walking out to the woods," Nate moans.

I pull in a breath. One of us has to be the voice of reason here. "You're not zombie-walking anywhere."

"How are you gonna stop it? We don't have medicine or helicopters or any of the high-tech gadgets the good guys need."

Dad's not around and the Crofts are definitely not gonna swoop in and save the day. There's no more time for wishing things were different. We need to find a solution without them.

"Who do the good guys call for help in the zombie movies, Nate?"

He scratches his chin. "Well, it depends. Sometimes there's a specialized zombie unit already in place . . . but that's in the more futuristic ones. The CDC usually comes around in most of 'em."

The Centers for Disease Control. Perfect. I whirl to the computer and do a search. It's time we got the big dogs involved. They'll come out to the woods and take care of this mess. Spray down everything remotely fungal. Close Vitaccino for good and give everybody in town pills or injections or something.

I find the number and dial. After going through a few automated options, I finally get a real person on the phone.

"Texas Center for Infectious Disease, this is John, how may I help you?" a monotone voice recites.

I look at Nate sprawled out on the couch. This is the moment things change. We're stopping Ophiocordyceps. Today. "I need to speak to someone in the fungal division."

There's a long pause.

"Hello?"

"I'm here," John responds in the same tired voice.

"Great, can you put me through to someone who handles hazardous fungi?" I pace the kitchen.

"I'm not sure I'm following. This is about a fungus?"

"That's right."

John sighs. "Tina works in the mycology department, but she's on maternity leave until next month. I can transfer you to Bryan, if you want."

"Someone is going to get hurt if you don't do something right away. There's a hostile fungi takeover going on in my town right now."

"Hostile takeover?" John suddenly sounds much more alert. "Are you talking about a public health threat in progress?"

"That's what I've been trying to tell you. Ophiocordyceps is dangerous. In fact, one man's already dead."

Nate meets my eye and nods enthusiastically.

"This isn't a joke?"

"No, sir. This threat is very real."

"I need to get your name, home address, and a call-back telephone number."

"My name's Magnolia Stone, but the real problem's happening down at Old Man Bell's place. I don't actually know the street address, but it's about two miles from town, past the railroad tracks where the paved road dies off."

There's some low voices in the background. When John speaks again his voice is urgent. "All right, miss, what's the nature of this threat and when will it be released?"

"Some of it's already been released. The spores just kind of shoot off into the air. It's not all that predictable. More could come any minute," I say, glad that John's finally starting to take my call seriously.

There's more murmuring. "Did someone ask you to make this call? Does the group you're working with have any demands?"

"Demands?" I ask, standing up a little straighter.

"Is there something these people want? Something we have to give them to stop the spread of the toxin?"

"People? You mean Ophiocordyceps?"

"We need you to talk with whoever is in charge. Tell them not to make a move or there will be serious consequences." There's a flurry of typing and shuffling papers in the background.

That's when I know. John doesn't understand that I'm talking about a super-freaky jungle fungus. "Wait. There's been a bit of a mix-up. I'm not with any group. There *isn't* any group. This is about a mutated fungus."

"But you said there was an imminent health threat?"

"There is. We've got a bad fungus problem here. It's infected my big brother and maybe my best friend, too." My voice speeds up as I try to push the words out before John calls out a SWAT team. "Sometimes Ezra's lips glow blue and if we don't do something, I'm afraid he might have spore clouds shoot out of his mouth soon. Plus, there's a whole deal with the local health-drink company and their secret ingredient, but that's another story."

"Your brother is blue?"

"Just his lips and not all the time. But he's got the same cough as the first man who died. And he keeps hanging out in the woods and moving around all slow and zombie-like."

There's another long pause. "I see what's going on here."

"You do?" I give Nate a thumbs-up. "How quick can you get a team out here?"

There's more chatter followed by what almost sounds like faint laughter. "I know summer break can get a bit boring and that prank calls are a real funny time killer, but they waste taxpayer dollars and take us away from serious issues. We've got actual work to do here, kid."

All the excitement floods out of me. John isn't sending backup. He's about to hang up on me. "I'm not pranking anyone. There really is a mutant fungus attacking my town."

"You had your fun, but the jig's up."

"If you'd just send a team, you'd know I'm not kidding. We really need your help!"

"Have a nice day and don't call here again until you're at least twenty-one." There's a moment of silence, then the repetitive drone of a disconnected call. I stare back at the receiver.

"I guess that means the CDC is out?" Nate asks.

"I'll think of something." I pace the floor and consider calling the state health department. But something tells me that won't go any better—especially if any of them remember the incident with Dad and the lab rats. Too bad the only adult who'd actually take me seriously is miles away. Probably making his own big discoveries while I'm stuck here trying to convince everybody that I'm not just some dumb kid making stuff up. The thing is if all these grown-ups would study a little bit more, they'd realize what I'm saying isn't so crazy. Nature can be cruel. It's filled with all sorts of everyday monsters. Vampire bats, mosquitos, and what about those wasps that lay their eggs inside caterpillars and make them explode when the larvae hatch?

The phone rings and I jump. "Maybe John changed his mind about sending help."

Nate flops his head back on the couch.

I grab the receiver. "Hello?"

"Hello, Magnolia. It's Mac Washington. Down at The Wormery."

"Oh, hey, Mac," I say, and slump onto a barstool. "How's it going?"

"Just fine and dandy. I'm calling to let you know there's been some happenings with the slime mold and stinkhorn samples. They've changed."

"Really?" I'd started to think the samples we left with Mac had turned out to be a dead end. I wonder for a split-second if some dog vomit slime mold and a stinky stalk are enough evidence to get the sheriff on board. I imagine holding up a mason jar with the stuff and trying to explain. Even in my head the sheriff looks confused. It'll never fly.

"I think you're gonna want to come and see it," Mac says. "It's really something."

Nate moans. "I can feel the pop mutating my innards. I'm zombifying one organ at a time."

Then again, sitting around here isn't doing much good. I grab my backpack and shove Dad's journal inside. "We'll be there in a half hour."

CHAPTER TWENTY-SIX

Other than Bubba Bass flipping his tail back and forth, The Wormery is quiet. Mac stands at the counter, hands folded like he's been frozen, waiting for us ever since his call. "Afternoon, kiddos."

"We got here as quick as we could," I say.

"You made good time. Come on back and I'll show you everything under the scope." Mac takes a few backward steps through the doorway.

Maybe Mac could call the sheriff for us. If a grown-up talks to him about the fungus, he just might be willing to take a patrol car out to the woods. If he saw the workers doing their sleepwalking routine, even he'd have to admit the woods were infected.

"Uh, Maggie," Nate calls. "I think you'd better take a look at this."

"Just a sec." I turn to Mac, who's lingering in the corner of the workroom. "Where are the samples you wanted to show us?"

"In that drawer over there." Mac points to a beat-up filing cabinet.

"Mags, I'm serious. Come here!" Nate hollers again.

"Just give it a pull," Mac says.

A drip of green runs down the side of the cabinet, and there's a funky smell. Like Elmer's glue mixed with pond water. I give the drawer a tiny tug. Fluorescent green fuzz bubbles out and sploshes down the sides like a glow-in-the-dark volcano erupting.

I scuttle back. The Wormery's infected. "We need to get out of here, Mac. Your place isn't safe."

"But you haven't even looked at the specimens under the scope," Mac says. His eyes are dull and his mouth droops slightly on one side. He shifts his body and I finally catch a glimpse of the back of him. A long, rope-like stalk protrudes from the nape of his neck. A dusty bulb the size of a baseball swells from the end. I stumble back, falling into a bin of fishing reels.

"You all right, Magnolia?" He shuffles closer.

I scramble to my feet, race past Mac, and push out the workroom door.

"There you are! You gotta see this." Nate motions to a wall coated in shimmery mushroom caps the color of green apple Kool-Aid.

"That's not the worst of it." I tug his arm. "Run!"

Mac lumbers after us, bumping into a display of fishing

poles and sending them crashing to the ground. "Magnolia? Nate? Don't run off just yet. I need to talk to ya."

Nate turns, his eyes landing on Mac. "*Ah!!!* What the—"

The bulb at the end of Mac's stalk pulses and a faint mist of spores drifts up.

"No time to talk," I say, and flip the sign in the front window from OPEN to CLOSED. We burst out the doors and I squat, yanking the laces from my sneakers. I tie the handles of the double doors together in a tight loop. "Mac is gonna need to stay put for a while."

We jump on our bikes and I steal a glance back at The Wormery. For the first time, I notice a luminous teal break in the ground. It's a foot wide and stretches from the drippy green puddle under the vending machine all the way to the side of the shop. Fleshy fungus sprouts out of the opening.

It wasn't just the stuff in the bags that made Mac sick. It was the Vitaccino seeping into the earth all around him. Just then, a splatter of white flies toward the glass and coats The Wormery's windows in a thick layer of spores.

We zoom away and a slow-motion video kicks off inside my head. Flashes of all the times Mac's offered up an ice-cold root beer on a hot day or told me all about a feather or bug I couldn't identify. He didn't deserve that stalk.

We ride until my legs are mush and my mouth is drier

than the Sahara. Up ahead, the late-afternoon sun glistens off Murphy's Pond. We just left a highly infectious area wearing no protection. My eyes meet Nate's, and he nods. We pedal right up to the banks, jump off our bikes, and leap into the brown water.

"I'm feeling itchy, Mags," Nate says between splashes of pond water. "I'm pretty sure one of those things is about to erupt out of the back of my head."

"Just keep washing." I dunk myself under, then grab a floating lily pad and scrub my hands and face.

Nate submerges himself for a solid thirty seconds. When he finally bursts to the surface, muddy streaks run down his face. "That was the freakiest thing I've ever seen. Can you imagine how famous I'd be if I'd gotten it on film?"

"I'm glad you didn't. I don't ever want to see any of that again." But even when I squeeze my eyes shut, the images are still there, like graffiti sprayed across my brain.

"We're seriously in deep dookie." Nate moves toward shallower water. "Mac's in full-on zombie mode. He totally called us there to spread his spores. The fungapocalypse is upon us!"

My throat feels thick, like I've swallowed down a cup of paste. "We should've warned him that Ophio was dangerous."

Nate wrings water from his T-shirt. "If you want to blame somebody, blame those Vitaccino jerks. They're the ones who knew about the fungus and coulda done something a long time ago instead of growing fields of the junk. We're just a couple of kids caught up in this mess."

"Maybe so, but if I'd called him and told him what we knew, Mac might still be okay."

Nate drops down onto a log along the shore. "Is this the moment where we admit defeat and wait for the end?"

If we walk away now, then Mac's on his own. And Ezra and the rest of the workers are still in danger. If we don't help them, they may have stalks growing out of their necks soon too. "People need us, Nate. Now we've got real-deal evidence of an outbreak. We're talking to the sheriff. The Wormery's all the proof we need."

We ride hard into downtown Shady Pines. No chitchat or stopping for air the whole way. Once the sheriff checks out the bait shop, there will be no denying that something has to be done.

We hit Main Street and are in luck. The sheriff's truck is pulled off on the side of the road, red lights flashing. Deputy Ronald leans in at the driver's-side window of a van parked in front of them.

"Looks like they're giving someone a ticket," Nate says.

"Whatever it is, it can wait."

"Sporemageddon trumps all," Nate says, then follows it up with a round of coughing that sets my heart to pounding. We've got no time to waste.

"Deputy Ronald!" He doesn't turn around. I eye the back of the van. The doors are open, and the sheriff is rustling around inside. "Sheriff Huxley?"

He glances over his shoulder but doesn't answer. He's cutting open a stack of boxes.

"There's been an incident at The Wormery," I say. "You need to get some hazmat suits and check it out. Mac Washington is in trouble. He's got a—"

"Mac'll have to wait," the sheriff drawls. "Shipment's gotta go out, but some of these here supplies ain't quite right." He reaches into a box and pulls out a green can, then calls, "Fellas, I could use a hand over here if you got a sec."

The deputy shuffles toward the back of the van, his face obscured by his wide-brim cowboy hat.

"You know, Mags, I just remembered I need to babysit the twins," Nate calls.

"Twins?" I turn toward Nate. Then I see the side of the van. The smiling woman holding a frosty can of Vitaccino.

The driver's-side door opens. A pair of dusty black boots steps out. "Hello there, Maggie. The officers are busy at the moment. Allow me to assist you." Albert Eldridge glides toward us. His jacket flutters, revealing a ribbed inside that looks just like a mushroom's gills. Puffs of swirling spores seep from the dark folds as he approaches.

"It's you." I skitter back. "What are you doing here?"

"We're preparing a shipment. But the recipe's been updated and some of these drinks don't have the right ingredients."

"Lemme guess, the new recipe is one hundred percent, not from concentrate, spore juice?" Nate asks.

Albert smiles and the edges of his mouth stretch wide across his cheeks. "Precisely."

"Did the Crofts tell you to do this?" I ask.

"Their assistance is unnecessary." Albert plucks a Vitaccino can from one of the boxes. He cracks it open and inhales. His face contorts like he's just breathed in a whiff of roadkill. He crushes the can, spraying out Vitaccino, and then launches the entire box halfway down the street. "Get rid of all of them."

The sheriff nods, and he and the deputy start tossing more boxes onto the street. Nate and I race to our bikes. Albert saunters after us. Frilly turquoise mushrooms sprout up on the road following his steps.

"I think it's safe to assume Vitaccino's under new management," Nate says as we wheel past the van.

"Our workforce is growing daily. Join us anytime," Albert calls, and kicks a box into the street. It barely misses my back tire.

In a matter of hours, everything has gone horribly, terribly, irrevocably wrong. Shady Pines is falling apart. I feel like I'm gonna be sick, but I'm too scared to quit pedaling and pull off the road. So I press one arm tight against my belly and steer one-handed.

We skid through the Raccoon Creek entrance and toss the bikes between our trailers. I'm panting from the hard ride home, but Nate's borderline wheezing. When he finally drops to his porch, his eyes are shiny. "This is way worse than I thought was possible, and I'm a guy who thinks a lot of bad stuff is possible."

I collapse next to him. My head's still trying to catch up with what my eyes just saw. I've spent years thinking I had a better grip on reality than Nate. Now I'm not so sure.

"That guy throws spores out like confetti at a Fourth of July parade," Nate says. "We can't win this one."

"We'll call the CDC again or the FBI or somebody," I say, but my voice is shaky and small. I think about the gleaming mushrooms in the woods. The clouds of spores swirling like dust devils. The moaning through the trees. Old Man Bell knew it was Albert. He knew what Albert was, and he was scared.

"It's too late for that. By the time they got here, we'd all be zombies."

If we give up, all of us—Ezra, Nate, me, the whole town—will end up like Mac. We have to come up with a new plan, but I don't know what. "You're worn out from the ride. Let's grab a snack and then we'll come up with something. We always do."

"This time's different, Mags."

"Come on, you know tons about zombie apocalypses, right? There's gotta be something in one of your books that can help."

Nate slumps against the porch. "I know enough to see the odds are against us. The zombie wasps got me. I drank the sporified Vitaccinos. Now I've got the cough and Albert Eldridge is swooping through town with his horde. We gotta face it, doomsday is at our door."

"We'll find a way to stop Albert."

"We're not superheroes, Mags. We're just a couple of kids from Raccoon Creek Trailer Park. Nothing's going to be all right." He stands, heading for his door.

CHAPTER TWENTY-SEVEN

t's not like Nate to give up in the face of danger. Maybe the zombie wasps and guzzling all that Vitaccino really did do something to his brain.

The cuckoo clock in the living room chirps five times. I peer down the hall for Ezra, but his light is off and his room is empty. I have a feeling I know exactly where he is, and it isn't good. I bolt the front door and push a chair against it.

I call Gramma's cell phone, but it goes straight to voice mail. She's not the best about keeping it charged but pretty good about listening to her messages. "Gramma, it's me. You need to come home right away. Don't go into town. Don't trust anyone. This is serious. I'll tell you everything when you get here."

I try Dad again but get his voice mail too. "I don't know when you'll hear this, but something bad's happened. There's a fungus called Ophiocordyceps. And this is gonna be hard to believe, but it turns people into zombies. Ezra's sick and so are a lot of other people. I wish you were here with me." I shake a bit of dried mud off my T-shirt. "I'm going to try to stop it. I think that's what you'd do. I hope I get it right."

My skin is clammy from the dip in Murphy's Pond. I strip down and crank the shower nearly as hot as it'll go. It stings, but if I can keep at it, maybe I can melt away all the terrible things that are reeling through my mind. I squeeze my eyes tight and imagine Dad coming through the door. Telling me he's got all the answers. The formula that fixes every broken, messed-up thing that's happening right now.

But the water runs cold and there's no knock on the door or phone ringing. I turn the faucet off. I'm shivering and alone.

I put on fresh clothes, then fall down on my bed. I shove my head under the pillow. This is really bad. And I'm scared. I don't have a team of doctors or even my own microscope. I can't fix this or save anybody. Nate was right. We are doomed.

I let the tears come until my pillow is wet against my cheeks. When I finally lift my head, the light in my room has faded to dingy gray. Lennox scampers up his terrarium glass and I give him a pinch of dried crickets. He licks his eyeball appreciatively.

There's a chirpy meow and Pascal slinks into the room.

"Hey." I kneel and scratch behind his tangerine-colored ears. He purrs. "Be glad you're a cat and don't have to worry about anything." I press my face into his long, silky fur. I wish I could go back in time six months. Back to when things made sense. Before Dad moved away and everything started to come apart.

Pascal's body suddenly tenses, and he releases a spitty hiss next to my ear. "What's wrong, boy?" His gaze locks on the carpet. A fuzzy brown spider the size of a quarter creeps across the floor. Pascal leaps from my lap.

I jump after him. "Don't touch that!"

Pascal pounces, and his jaws snap around the spider before I can grab him. Wriggling legs protrude from his mouth. "Pascal! Spit that out!"

Instead of dropping the spider, he bites down again and with a few ferocious chomps, swallows it.

"Oh, Pascal, you shouldn't have!" I moan as he licks the fur around his mouth.

He looks up at me with such pride that I can't hold back a slight smile. There was no long skinny stalk that I could see or explosion of powdery spores. The spider is dead and we're okay. Pascal slinks around my legs, his tail held regally high.

I scratch the back of his neck. "You're pretty pleased with yourself, aren't you?"

His golden eyes are filled with satisfaction. With

another meow, he slinks off down the hall. I stand and peer around my room. My eyes land on the sun catcher hanging by the window. Fragments of forest green light splay over my bedspread. The glass *Hemaris diffinis* floats daintily above the colored circles and rocks. Dad's not here, but he's not altogether gone, either. I can still hear his voice in my head. He wouldn't quit. He'd come up with a plan. Maybe people would say it's crazy or would never work, but it would.

I pull Dad's journal out of my backpack and flip through the pages. There are notes on his failed hydroponic garden, half-baked plans for a homemade beehive, and a sketch of the rats in the Vitaccino supply. Dad's run into plenty of problems, but he always kept going.

I pace the floor. Dad says science is more than formulas and charts. It's curiosity and answering the questions that are right in front of you. I've got a huge question right now—how can I save Shady Pines—and I need a really big answer.

I glance at my desk. The envelope of cash from the board is still sitting there, just waiting to be spent. I grab the bills and shove them into my pocket. It's not exactly an answer, but like Gramma says, "You gotta play the cards you're dealt."

CHAPTER TWENTY-EIGHT

I pour a glass of orange juice and grab a cheese stick from the deli drawer. A highly infectious mutant fungus is galloping through town and I've got a pocketful of money but no idea how to stop it. I munch and pace.

I swallow down another bite of cheese and open the journal to a fresh page. I jot down everything I know about the outbreak. When I'm finished, five pages are covered with purple ink. It's all a hodgepodge of puzzle pieces that don't quite fit together.

Things I Know About Ophiocordyceps
Prefers humid biome
Infection rate varies
Human symptoms: cough, occasional glowing,
    slow-walk, obeying A.E.
The first victim: Old Man Bell

I circle that last bit.

Bell knew about the threat and he was scared. But up until a couple of weeks ago, nobody was glowing or hacking out spores. Something changed when he died. Everything that was locked up in those woods got out.

From my research, I know different treatments work on different fungi. Maybe I could go to Goodman's Pharmacy and buy every anti-fungal cream and spray they've got. With the Merit Award cash, I have enough money to get a pretty good supply. I chew my lip. I've got a feeling it'll take more than a squeeze of Lotrimin to take down a guy who drips mushrooms when he walks.

I rake through the journal again. As I do, my eyes land on the word *"Geronimo"*—the name painted on Old Man Bell's crop duster. Every day for years, he flew that plane over the woods. The day he died that all stopped.

I sit up bolt straight. That's it.

Old Man Bell must have been spraying the land with some kind of fungicide. That way Ophio stayed locked behind his NO TRESPASSING signs. I push away from the table and race out my front door.

I dash up Nate's porch steps and ring the bell. As I wait, there's a low growl. Glory rustles out from the bushes. Her long, floppy ears radiate cerulean and white foam drips from her jowls. She takes a slow step my way.

"Shoo," I say, waving a hand in her direction. Of all the scary things I've seen today, a lazy basset hound is the least of my worries.

She gives another half-hearted growl.

"No, ma'am. That's bad manners."

Glory puts her tail between her legs then trudges down the porch heading for the Raccoon Creek exit. If all the infected creatures are that easy to handle, tonight will be a breeze.

The Fulton twins finally answer the door decked out in orange capes and oversize work boots. "We're not 'pposed to open the door by ourselves no more. But we looked through the peeping hole and sawed you," Collin says.

"Thanks, guys." I poke my head around them. "Nate here?"

"We wanted him to toast our waffles, but he didn't. He's being a toot-face. He said if you came to tell you he was sick."

I force a smile. "No worries. I'll get him up."

Benny spreads his little arms wide, blocking the doorway. "He's sick."

The twins look up at me with big, stubborn eyes. They're tough negotiators, but if there's one thing I know, it's the way to the Fulton heart. "If you let me in, I'll toast your waffles. Extra syrup and butter."

They eye each other, then swing the front door wide open. After I fix a hulking stack of waffles, I stalk down the hall to Nate's room. It's dark inside, but I can still spot a Nate-size lump in the middle of his messy bed. I click on the light. "Get up."

"I'm choosing to use my remaining hours in a matter I see fitting," he mumbles from beneath the covers.

"Sporemageddon hasn't won yet. I've got a plan."

"It's time we face the inevitable, Mags. We are the last of humanity and these are the end days."

"Will you get out of bed already?" I toss a sneaker at the Nate lump.

"Ouch! Don't you have any respect for the gravely ill?"

I push my hands through my hair. Collin was right. Nate is being a toot-face. My eyes drift to a pile of *Midnight Kingdom* comics spread over his floor. Desperate times call for desperate measures. I clear my throat and don my best movie announcer voice. "Would Brigadier Ajax give up in the face of death? Would he let his people and his good name be defeated by a monster of unknown origins and unfathomable capabilities?"

The blankets shift and Nate peeks out from under his comforter. "A tribe of hostile robotic dolphins once dipped him into hot lava."

"And did he give up?" I ask, hoping my general knowledge of *Midnight Kingdom* plots holds true.

"No way, that's when he developed his seventeenth superpower—heat resistance. He jumped out of that volcano totally unscathed. It was epic." Nate sits up, looking suddenly reenergized. "Ajax took down the dolphins' evil praying mantis emperor and made the rest of the robots repair his spaceship."

I put one hand on my hip. "Well, that's what we're going to do."

"But we don't even have a spaceship," he says, flipping his curls out of his eyes.

I pull the bills out of my pocket and slap them against my hand. "But we do have five hundred big ones, and that's nearly as good."

"How's that going to stop the outbreak?"

"Remember how Old Man Bell used to spray down his woods with that crop duster? My theory is the plane was filled with a fungicide that kept Ophio from spreading to the rest of town. Then when Bell died and quit spraying, it got out."

Nate wrinkles his forehead. "But you saw that weird moth with the stalk before he died."

I pause. He's got a point. "Maybe it slipped out. I don't know, but right now the crop duster is our best bet."

"So . . . you want us to fly a plane?" Nate asks, looking intrigued. "I mean, I've played some pilot video games. I guess I could probably—"

"We're not flying anything. We just need the fungicide. We could always snoop around Bell's cabin for some, but the plane seemed like a less creepy option."

"Not the ghost hut," Nate murmurs with a slight shudder.

"The crop duster it is, then," I say. "The only tricky part is figuring out a way to get the fungicide out of the plane and onto everything that's infected."

"So a siphon pump, for starters."

I tilt my head. "A what?"

"You know, the thing that's gonna get the fungus killer out of the plane and into something else." Nate shrugs like the whole thing's totally obvious.

"Right. I hadn't really thought that far out yet." I pick at the hem of my T-shirt. Finding some random pump on short notice could be a problem.

Nate gives a sideways grin.

"What? Why are you smiling?"

"No reason. It's just kinda nice knowing something you don't."

"How exactly do you know anything about siphons, anyway?"

"Remember when Benny poured lemonade into my dad's gas tank on Christmas Eve and I couldn't go with you to the Sunny Day Nursing Home party?"

"Your dad was super ticked."

"Yeah, well, he made me watch YouTube videos until I figured out how to fix it. It was pretty easy. Just had to raid his supplies for some PVC pipes, duct tape, and a plumbing hose."

"You wouldn't happen to still have that siphon lying around the house, would you?"

Nate shakes his head. "Nope."

My shoulders fall.

"It's not in the house. It's in my dad's woodshed."

"You're just full of surprises, aren't you?" I smile, glad that he's back on the team.

"I'm a regular international man of mystery."

"You so are. Now let's get moving."

Nate jumps out of bed and grabs his camcorder off his nightstand. As we hurry through the living room, Benny pops his head up from the couch. "Whatcha doing?"

Oh no. The twins. Somehow, I'd completely forgotten that we can't just leave a pair of diabolical three-year-olds home alone.

"Ah dang." Nate grimaces. Clearly the boys had slipped his mind too. "You think we can take them with us?"

"To the epicenter of the fungal outbreak?"

"I guess not," Nate says. "I can't leave them alone. They'll burn the place down, or worse."

I need Nate. This was our mission from the beginning. He's the para to my normal. The action to my sit-and-think. I can't do this without him. I plop down on the couch next to Collin, all the adrenaline of the breakthrough seeping from me.

Nate grabs the kitchen phone. A second later he's talking

to somebody on the other end. "Hey, bro, any chance you can do me an ultra-huge favor?" Nate grins. "You're a true hero."

Fifteen minutes later, there's a rumbling out front and a skinny, dark-haired boy in ripped jeans and a muscle shirt waltzes in the front door. It's Nate's cousin, Ricky. "What's up, dude?"

"Just saving the world with Mags," Nate answers.

Collin and Benny straddle themselves around each of Ricky's legs. He laughs and tussles their hair. "Saving the world, huh?"

I nod. "That's actually pretty spot on."

Ricky glances around the place. "You guys got any frozen corn dogs?"

Nate wriggles his eyebrows. "Half a box."

"Then I'm all set." Ricky flops down on the couch and grabs the TV remote. The twins rest their messy heads of hair on his shoulders.

"Keep the twins inside, will ya, Ricky? There's some nasty junk going around."

"You got it, bro. We're going to binge-watch old TMNT and eat our weight in junk," Ricky says. The twins exchange high fives.

"Where to?" Nate asks as we head out the door.

"We suit up, then head to the armory."

Nate arches an eyebrow. "Shady Pines has an armory?"

"Better known as Goodman's Pharmacy."

CHAPTER TWENTY-NINE

We assemble our homemade hazmat suits, then snag the siphon pump from the woodshed.

On the way out of the trailer park, I glance up at the tree house and notice the old oak it's built in is covered in bulbous blue growths. Putting Albert's jelly up there definitely didn't help the situation.

We jump on our bikes and ride downtown. The streetlamps are just flicking on as we arrive. Normally there's a steady trickle of people coming and going, but tonight the sidewalks are empty and no cars are parked at the meters. Nate leans his bike against the side of Goodman's. "What exactly are we looking for in here?"

"We're striking back, and we need combat gear." I grab a cart and make a beeline for the seasonal aisle. I lurch to a stop in front of a display of half a dozen high-powered squirt guns.

Nate's eyes sparkle. "The MegaBlaster 3000."

"Let's load 'em up," I say, grabbing an armful. "Two for each of us, plus a couple more just in case."

When we've cleared out the display, Nate holds up a bag of army-green water grenades. "What do you think?"

"This is war. Throw them in. All of them."

At the checkout, I slap two of the hundred-dollar bills on the counter and say a line I've always dreamed of using: "Keep the change."

Kiki blinks back at me, her eyes dull as dirty pennies. "Whatcha doing with all the squirt guns?" She hands me a bag, her fingers flickering like the neon lights in front of Banjo's Pool Hall.

The fungus is spreading through town fast.

I grab Nate's arm. "Time to go!"

We race out to the street and strap our gear onto the back of our bikes with a couple of bungee cords we swiped from the woodshed. As we pass the sheriff's department, a voice calls after us. "It's not safe for you youngins to be runnin' the streets at night. Come on inside." Sheriff Huxley, trailed by Deputy Ronald and Kiki, shuffle toward us in a horizontal line.

"Don't you want your receipt?" Kiki calls, stretching out her glow-in-the-dark arm. "No refunds without a receipt."

I start to pedal and notice Nate holding his camcorder, filming the whole thing. "Your Internet stardom can wait.

We've got sporemageddon to wrangle!" I yell.

Nate slides his camera into his backpack. "You looked fantastic saying that last line. Just fantastic."

As we pump away, we pass the fire station and my feet lose their grip on the pedals. A fleshy cyan mushroom as tall as one of the twins rises up from the station's lawn. A cyclone of spores whirls out from the top. I yank my bandanna over my nose and pedal harder.

As we reach the forest, the moon casts silvery light onto a dark line of trees. We grab two blasters each, abandon our bikes, and start out on foot.

My garbage bag suit sticks to my skin and sweat rolls down my back. We follow a path of shimmering sapphire mushrooms. It's like someone's rolled out a neon carpet leading us straight to the heart of the forest. A lone owl hoots as we dodge thorny brambles and ghostly oaks draped in moss.

Up ahead, something white flutters from a pile of dried leaves. I kneel. It's crumpled-up papers held in place by a silver cell phone.

"What is all that?" Nate asks.

I click a button on the phone. An image of Ezra, Jack, and Zion appears on the home screen. "It's Ezra's phone." I smooth out the papers. "And the pages Ezra tore out of Dad's journal."

"Your bro's throwing out his stuff in the woods. That doesn't seem like a good sign."

I peer down at the papers and read one of Dad's entries. It's dated six months ago.

> Today I found a box of green powder waiting for processing. A rat family with some weird growths had made its home in there. I tried to dump them outside, but they made a break for it before I could catch them. I told A.E., but he says not to worry. He'll take care of everything. Something seems off about it. I think I'll run a couple of tests of my own.

At the bottom of the page there's a sketch I never really noticed before. Rats with squiggles at the back of their heads. The rats, Albert, the fungus. They're all connected. "No wonder Ezra didn't want anyone to see these pages."

Nate peers over my shoulder. "Ophio was working its charm on him already."

"Dad knew something was wrong at the factory. If the Crofts hadn't fired him, he might've put the pieces together."

"Sure would be nice if he could tell us how to take down the ol' Spore King."

For a moment I imagine Dad tromping through the woods by my side. He's decked out in the same trash bag suit and goggles. We're stalking through the night, Mega-

Blasters hoisted on our shoulders. We're not scared or lost or confused. He's with us and we know we're gonna win.

My boots crunch over fallen twigs and the daydream fades away. I slip Ezra's phone and Dad's crumpled pages into my backpack. We walk in silence until we come to the downed crop duster. Moss and vines twist around the plane, making it look like a relic from some long-forgotten war. I just hope it's got enough oomph left in it to help us win this battle. "So how exactly does this work?" I ask.

"All we gotta do is connect one end of the hose to the fungicide tank and the other to the MegaBlasters. Gravity will do the rest," Nate says.

"Where do you think the tank might be?" I walk around to the nose of the plane.

"It's not all that big. It can't be that hard to find," Nate says, then gives a dry, raspy cough.

"You okay?"

"So far, so good." Nate squats beneath one wing and eyes the ground. "Hey, remember all those mushrooms that were over here before?"

"I guess so." I shrug. It's not like mushrooms are any big surprise around here anymore.

"They're all shriveled up now. Plus, there's a bunch of gunk that looks like black Tic Tacs."

"Ew." I peer under the plane. Sure enough, the mushrooms look like they got stuck in a dehydrator and turned to fungus jerky. "Some of the fungicide must have dripped down and killed them off. That's a good sign."

Nate fiddles around the bottom of the plane for a few minutes, grunting and muttering to himself. Then he slides his head out. "I found the tank, but I can't get the cap off. Can you find me a rock or something I can bang against it and loosen it up?"

I circle the plane but there're only leaves and sticks. A few yards away there's an opening in the side of an earthy hill, like a miniature cave. I trot over and dip my head in. The walls are low enough that I have to crouch, but its plenty wide. As I shuffle around, I bump into something warm. It squeaks and I scuttle back.

A storm of black shapes flaps out of the cave. Hundreds of furry masses whirl upward, surrounding us with wings beating in a wild dance.

"Bats!" Nate shrieks. "Bats are as bad as spiders!"

They squeal as they soar over us, blocking out everything except the view of their leathery wings. My trash bag shifts, then flaps against my chest as a writhing bat flutters underneath. Reports of rabid bats infecting unsuspecting hikers whip through my mind. That and an image of a ghoulish vampire straight out of a horror movie. I screech and spin around in a circle until I shake the thing out.

My trash bag has a three-inch tear down one side, and there's bat guano on my rain boots. But the sky is finally clear and the bats' squeaks have faded away.

"Are they gone?" Nate peeks out from behind his hands.

"I hope so," I say and scrape my boots against a rock.

"This forest needs to be burned to the ground." Nate grabs a stone from the mouth of the cave, then peeks under the plane. After a thorough inspection, he drops under the crop duster again. There's a few seconds of banging, then Nate announces he's got the cap off. "Hand me the pump. I don't want to be under here any longer than I have to."

A cloud shifts over the moon, and the forest grows darker. A sawing sound drifts from the trees, like cicadas only deeper and louder.

Nate pokes his head out. "Do you feel that buzzing?"

"There's a sound, but I don't feel anything."

Nate shakes his head. "My bones feel like magnets and something in the woods is yanking on them."

All I feel is the hot stickiness of the trash bag against my sweaty skin. "Let's just fill up the blasters and get going."

Nate pushes himself up. "I'm gonna check it out."

"What? No way! We need to stay together." But Nate's already marching down a path sprinkled with aqua fungi. The trees quiver and there's a whooshing sound like a jet taking off. "Nate? Is that you?"

The dazzling lights of the forest suddenly disappear. I'm in total darkness when I hear his voice.

"You've returned at last. Welcome."

CHAPTER THIRTY

In the clearing up ahead, Nate stands stock-still. I jog after him. "Nate, come back!"

He doesn't move.

Albert Eldridge steps into a sliver of moonlight. "I'm so glad you've decided to join us."

I duck behind a clump of rotting tree limbs, pulse pounding.

Nate squeezes one fist. "I'm not joining anything. You're a bad guy. A really, really bad guy."

"Bad?" Albert slinks closer. "There is no good or bad. Only survival or extinction."

I can't decide between racing to Nate or sneaking back to the plane and filling up the first blaster. So I stay put, eyes darting from Nate to the plane.

"People have stalks growing out of their heads." Nate shuffles backward, his rain boots bumping over gnarly brambles. "That's not a positive thing, sir."

Albert inhales and the leaves on the trees seem to draw

closer to him. "You still don't understand, but you will. The world needs our kind."

"All right, well that's just creepy. And, uh, news flash: You're not a fungus. You're a dude."

"Since I met Ophio, everything has changed. Now I'm a host to something new. Working as one for the common good."

"And what's that? Turning everybody into a bunch of zombified mushroom people? 'Cause nobody wants any part of that. So why don't you just haul your moldy rumpus out of here?"

Wind whips through the trees and their long, leafy boughs rattle. I look toward the crop duster and wonder if I can make a break for it and grab the blaster without Albert noticing. I raise one foot to tiptoe back but I stumble and fall. I feel around with my gloves. A vine grips my ankle in a snug loop. I scratch at the ropey coil, but it only seems to squeeze tighter. A panicky feeling churns in my stomach. The whole forest is turning against us.

"There is no need to say more." Albert trudges toward Nate. "You've already taken the first step of initiation."

First step of initiation? Nothing about that sounds good.

"What are you talking about?" Nate asks, his voice more scared than angry.

I peek through the branches. Albert's eyes glint in the darkness. "You can feel it. A tickle in the back of your throat.

A tingling in your hands. The whispers. Faint now, but they'll get louder. Rising and rising until they're all you hear."

"I don't know what you're talking about." Nate's words come out thin. I want to run to him. To tell him that it's a lie; there won't be any tingling or whispers. That Albert is making it all up. But as I look at Nate, I catch a faint pulsing blue in his balled-up fists.

It's happening. One by one, the Spore King is picking off the people I care about most. I need ammo. Now. I tear through the first bit of vine around my ankle.

But Albert suddenly takes a step back into the dense trees and away from the clearing. There's a low murmur of voices up ahead. "We have company. Our little talk can wait." There's a blur of white and he's gone.

If we've got more infected workers closing in, I need to hurry. I rip off the last loop of the vine and race back to the plane. I grab a few water grenades and connect the first to the end of the hose. "Maggie," Nate calls, and there's a stirring of branches.

"I'm here!"

Nate rushes back and skids into me. "You got those blasters filled? I know a target that needs to be sprayed down, pronto."

"Not yet, but I've got a couple of grenades," I say, dropping them into my backpack. Just then a twig snaps behind us. We both whirl around.

There's a smudge of yellow, then we're surrounded. But it's not who I expected. At least ten people in bright yellow hazmat suits and heavy boots crunch toward us.

"Step away from the plane," a voice orders, and then pulls off the hazmat mask. It's Lydia Croft. "I see you children can't seem to stop meddling in my private affairs."

"Shady Pines is covered in mutant fungus," I say, grabbing one of the empty MegaBlasters.

"The town is going to be just fine. We'll have everything under control in no time. Now drop those water toys. You're making a mess of things." Lydia motions to her team and they march our way.

"Nothing is fine," I say. "Mac Washington has a stalk growing out of his skull, the fire department has a mushroom cyclone in its front yard, and the sheriff is working for the Spore King!"

"The Spore King?" Lydia's eyes shift to a cloud of luminous dust swirling in the shadows. "You're getting yourself too worked up, child. Some of our regular maintenance is a little off schedule with Bell's death, but we're taking care of it."

After everything I've seen, there's no way I trust the Crofts to handle this. They may have the right gear, but they're about as dependable as a pack of black widow spiders.

"No offense," Nate chimes in, "but you've done a pretty stinktastic job of handling it so far. Only a crazy person would add freaky jungle fungus to their soda pop."

At that, Charles Croft breaks away from the rest of the group. "You don't know the first thing about running a business. That fungus has doubled our profits. One taste and customers are loyal for life."

Nate snorts. "Loyal? Try zombified."

Lydia tosses a dismissive hand in the air. "Absurd. I drink a case a week and I'm as healthy as can be."

"Well, maybe nobody's told you, but your company's changed its management. And the new boss has a brand-spanking-new formula."

"That's ridiculous. No one's replacing me," Lydia snaps. "Charles! Bobby! Someone get these kids into the van!"

Two men grab Nate and one heads for me. I dodge under an arm and make a break toward Nate, but someone snags the straps of my backpack and I stumble. My blaster falls to the ground. I whirl around, swinging my bag, but a bulky man with a handlebar mustache already has a death grip on my wrist.

"Please! My brother's out there," I shout. "Let us help. We can spray stuff too."

Lydia fluffs her silver hair. "Tempting. But no. We have a national order to ship and the last thing we need is you two stirring up trouble."

I keep kicking and wriggling, but it doesn't do any good. The team drags us to a Vitaccino van parked in a clearing. One of the men yanks open the back door. The air inside is muggy and smells like corn syrup.

Nate grips the top of the van. "It's, like, a hundred degrees in there. You want us to suffocate or something?"

"You'll survive." The team shoves us in, slams the door, and stomps away. We're all alone and it's pitch black.

I fish my flashlight out of my backpack and shine it around. On both sides of the van there's a small sliding window. I push open the one closest to me and try to poke my head out, but can only fit my nose and chin. At least we can get air. I point the light at a wall separating the back of the van from the front seat. It looks pretty solid. My flashlight flickers, then goes out. "Guess it's gonna be a little dark."

"I don't think that's our biggest problem," Nate says.

I turn. His whole face glows sapphire blue.

CHAPTER THIRTY-ONE

Nate tugs off his gloves. "I need that fungicide, Mags."
I reach for one of the grenades in my backpack.
Then I stop, remembering when Albert poured the
jelly on the fungus and it sizzled up. "What if it's
not safe? What if it hurts you?"

"I'm already messed up. We don't have anything to lose."

He's probably right. I should throw the grenade at him.
Stopping the outbreak is what we came to the woods to
do. But I just can't bring myself to start with Nate. "Let's
see if we can get out of the van first."

"Fine. But if one of those stalks starts sprouting out the
back of my head, promise me you'll launch every bit of
mushroom killer you've got at me."

"I promise."

Nate sighs. "If I hadn't drank all those Vitaccinos, this
wouldn't be happening."

"We'd still be stuck in the back of this van. It'd just be
a bit darker."

Nate leans against one wall. "You would've put it together the second you saw all that fizzling green foam."

"You saw it fizzle green before you drank it?"

"I was thirsty. I don't always think things through. I just do stuff." Nate shakes his head. "You've got all your big plans to be some amazing scientist. And me? We both know I can't really grow up to be an alien robot hunter like Brigadier Ajax. That stuff is make-believe. I'm probably gonna end up being some wacked-out conspiracy theorist posting weird junk on the Internet for the rest of my life."

I smile. "Posting weird junk on the Internet is pretty much your dream."

"That's true." He peers down at his gleaming fingers. "Assuming I make it that long."

I slide over to Nate and put my gloved hands around his. "Of course you're going to make it. Can you imagine how boring my life would be without you? I'd probably end up ironing Gramma's dish towels all day with no one to talk to except Pascal. And he only has so much patience for my science."

Nate grins. "He'd probably poop on your research just to shut you up."

"Definitely. Cats are petty like that."

"And nobody takes poo-covered research seriously."

"They really don't," I say, and rest my head against the

side of the van. The air's so thick it feels like I'm inhaling molasses. It even has a buzz to it.

I glance at the window. A bee creeps along the opening. It pulses aquamarine. I stand to swat it away, but the hum gets louder. One by one, a growing army of bees, moths, and beetles coat the glass and make their way into the van. I scuttle back.

"Mags?" Nate whimpers. "Please tell me there's no spiders in that mess of nightmares."

"There's no spid—"

Just then a dark mass wriggles across the glass and crawls in. It's a fist-size orb-weaver spider with yellow stripes zigzagging down its sides. A long, skinny bean sprout rises from its head.

"We need to get out of here," I say. "Right now."

"Spider!" Nate squeals. "Not okay! NOT OKAY!"

I drop to my back and start kicking the wall that separates us from the front of the van. The combination of trash bag suit, heat, and stomping makes me light-headed.

Something tickles the back of my hand. I look down. Black and gold fuzzy body. Paper-thin wings. Stalk. It's the bumblebee moth I once hoped would lead me to scientific glory. But now I know its third antenna isn't an antenna at all, but a spore-filled weapon. And from the size of it, I'd say it's ready to burst any minute.

I start kicking again and Nate joins in, his face glistening with a layer of sweat. The wall doesn't budge.

"Why are we doing this? It's made of steel," Nate pants.

I give another kick and the bumblebee moth glides into the air, its wings brushing my swim goggles as it goes. I pull the handkerchief over my nose, even though it makes it harder to breathe. White powder falls from the stalk onto the cloth. I hold my breath and the inside of the van blurs. My legs give way and drop to the floor with a thump. Tiny white stars flick at the sides of my vision.

Nate quits kicking too and lies crumpled on his side. "This is it, isn't it?"

I don't have enough air to answer him. The sawing of the insects drowns out everything.

As I drift into the darkness, there's a metallic creak. A gust of air flows into the van and light spills over us.

"Nathaniel," a voice hums. "Join us."

I turn. The back doors of the van are wide open. But there's no one there. Only a cloud of turquoise insects in the vague shape of a man. The wind stirs and the cloud blows apart until all that's left is the moonlit woods.

We crawl out and collapse on the dirt. I pull my bandanna down and suck in the fresh air. It's hot and humid but at least there's plenty of it.

After several big gulps, I sit up. Nate's got a far-away look in his eye like he's listening to distant music . . . or voices only he can hear.

"Let's see if we can round up those MegaBlasters," I say.

Nate stands, but his steps are slow and wobbly. When we make it back to the crop duster, the Vitaccino crew is gone but so are our MegaBlasters. Only the siphon pump remains, dangling from the crop duster like a flung-out spaghetti noodle.

"I've still got the pack of grenades," I say. "We can fill them up while we're here." I drop to my knees and start connecting a grenade to the hose.

Nate kicks at the dirt. "Those stinkin' bats have really nastied up this place."

I push a few of the little black pellets of bat guano away with the side of my boot and try to focus on the grenades. As I fill, Nate paces, alternating between dramatic sighs and comments like, "I can feel my bones fungifying!" It's oddly comforting. As long as he's being theatrical, I know he's still mostly himself. I get half a dozen grenades filled and stuffed into my backpack before there's a murmur of nearby voices.

"Which gang of jerk-faces do you think that is? Spore King Army or Vitaccino Hazmats?" Nate asks.

"Let's find out." I grab my bag and we creep past scrubby bushes and fallen tree limbs. We come to a grassy ridge and peer down at the mushroom field below.

"The national order is all that matters," Lydia says to

the hazmat team circled around her. "We need the workers picking at full speed."

"What about Albert?" Superintendent Silverton asks.
"You think he's still hiding out in the woods somewhere?"

"It doesn't matter. If he shows up, he's fired," Lydia
answers. "He's been making trouble for far too long."

A swirling gust lifts my hair and the mushrooms in
the field flicker, then go dark again. Nate shakes his head.
"We know where this is going."

Lydia spins around. "Albert? Is that you?"

The forest moans as Albert Eldridge glides out from its
depths, his jacket billowing behind him. "In the flesh . . .
or whatever is left."

CHAPTER THIRTY-TWO

Nate and I duck behind a tangle of vines. We've got a view of the whole field from here but are safely tucked out of sight.

"Albert?" Lydia flicks two fingers, signaling for the hazmat team to come close. "You don't sound like yourself."

"I've undergone some changes." Neon veins spring up in the earth between Albert and the hazmat team. Glistening light ripples through the woods in rivers of electric color.

Charles Croft gapes at the ground. "What? How are you doing that?"

"I knew you'd been a little out of sorts . . . but this is something else altogether," Lydia murmurs.

"I have you to thank." A musty smell wafts up from the ground and I pinch my nose. "The day you sent me here to dispose of the rats, I met Ophio. It's made me a new man."

Charles whistles, and the men in yellow suits form a

half circle around him and Lydia. "We've got a business to run. We're putting an end to your little freak show. After that, you can find yourself a new job. You're finished here."

"This is only just beginning." He tilts his head and Ezra, along with the rest of Albert's minions, emerge from the woods. "Together we will usher in an entirely new species. Part fungus, part man."

Charles slowly shakes his head. "You're completely insane."

"Seeing is believing." Albert raises one hand and his workers take a step toward the Crofts. Ezra's eyes are glazed and there's a blank expression on his face.

This has gone too far. I need Ezra to snap out of his trance. Dad always had this way of saying our names whenever one of us was in a mood. No matter what, it'd smooth things over. I spring from our hiding place. "Ezra!"

Nate jumps up after me. "I don't think that's a good plan!" he whisper-yells.

"Ezra!" I call again. But I don't sound like Dad. I sound screechy and panicked and small.

Lydia whirls toward me and Nate. "You two are the peskiest children I've ever known!"

Ezra doesn't glance our way. His skin shines a swamp-water green and his hair is ashy with a layer of powder. I press my handkerchief tight around my nose. "You've got to fight it, Ezra!"

"The time for fighting is over," Albert says, his translucent blue eyes falling on me.

"You need medicine, sir," I say. "You could get well again. Go back home."

"The forest is my home now," Albert answers. "And my family are all who join me here." He inhales and the veins in the ground crack wider. Long-limbed fungi the shape of sea crabs sprout from the crevasses.

"That fungus has rotted your brain." Charles scrambles away from the mushrooms as his team lugs an industrial-size hose through the woods.

"I wouldn't speak that way if I were you." Albert's workers march toward the Crofts' crew.

"There's something wrong with the connection, sir," one of the men in yellow suits says, giving the hose a shake.

"Fix it. Now!" Charles snaps.

"How unfortunate." Albert smiles, a cloud of spores spinning from his finger.

I dump the grenades out of my backpack and grab two. I can't stand by and let everyone get infected. Even if they're bad guys. I hurl both grenades at Albert's head. They explode and white foam coats his face. I pelt his torso with two more grenades. Fizzy white bubbles run down his chest.

He drops to his knees. "It burns!"

"Why did you have to go snooping around, Albert?

If you'd just eliminated the rats like we told you, you'd be fine. You've only got yourself to blame," Lydia says, giving Albert an "I told you so" glare.

Just then, the man with the handlebar mustache emerges from the woods. "The hose is fixed, sir. This punk disconnected it." He's dragging Nate behind him.

"Nate? Why would you do that?" But as the words leave my mouth I know the answer. Nate's eyes twitch from me to Albert's horde.

He wants to join them. He wants to follow Albert.

"Spray them. All of them," Lydia says, coming to Charles's side.

Albert sits in a crumpled heap, but the team tugs the hose toward him anyway. A blast of white squirts out, blanketing Albert and the others in liquid foam. The air is white with vapor. I race toward Ezra, but I can't find him in the cloud of fungicide. I can't find anyone.

After what feels like an eternity, the spray runs dry. The air clears and the men drag the hose back like a dead snake. Everything is still. Bodies are sprawled everywhere. I'm not sure if Nate's down on the ground or if he's managed to escape to the woods.

The fungicide might not have killed them, but nobody's moving. Who knows what kind of shape they'll be in when they wake? They might never be the same again. "We need to help them!"

But Lydia and her team keep moving, not paying me a bit of attention.

There's shuffling as the hazmat team moves through the field. "Clean this up," Lydia orders. "And get the girl out of here."

As one of the Vitaccino goons approaches, the ground under my feet vibrates. The wind whips through the trees and the light of the mushrooms quivers.

Albert Eldridge rises to his feet. He gives himself a shake and frothy white clouds roll off his shoulders.

Charles takes a step back. "Impossible."

"To survive one must adapt," Albert answers. "The weapons that once killed the fungus have grown dull and rusty."

"Anti-microbial resistance," Lydia murmurs.

Albert snaps his fingers and one by one the workers rise. Ezra, Zion, Jack, and the others slog to Albert's side. Fungicide drips off their arms and legs like soapy foam. "Bell should have noticed weeks before his death, but the old man underestimated Ophio. When the children came, Bell failed to properly suit up. He didn't expect an attack. A fatal mistake."

I've heard of antibiotics not working anymore because the bacteria became resistant to the medicine. I guess fungi can do the same thing.

"I'm not going to let you destroy our family's legacy."

Lydia picks up the empty hose and shakes it at Albert. Bits of white fling out from the nozzle.

"The time for surrender has arrived." Albert raises his arms and a piercing squeak fills the air. From the shadows, a black swarm scurries out. Dark masses with ropey tails and fur mottled with brilliant green flood toward the Crofts and their lackeys. Rats. Hundreds and hundreds of rats. Long, skinny stalks bloom from the back of every skull.

Something hits my foot and I scuttle back. Tiny claws snag at my rain boots as a rat bolts up my leg. I grab the tail and hurl it away.

The rats scramble over the Crofts' team until each yellow suit is completely covered. Like the locusts that swarm in summertime, the rats gnaw through the suits and strips of cloth and rip away plastic. In a matter of seconds, they've shredded the suits to rags.

Albert claps his hands and the rats draw back with shrill squeaks and disappear into the forest. "Now!" Albert opens his mouth and a whirling spore cloud spins out.

"Wait, Albert!" Lydia shrieks, tearing at a vine that's wrapped itself around her ankle.

The rest of the yellow suits turn to run, but the branches all around them shudder, bringing their limbs together like prison bars. Albert rises, growing taller and taller, like he's more spore cloud than man.

I race from the field and duck behind a thick tree trunk.

White blasts from his mouth, coating everything in sight with spores. My throat tightens. Nate was right. He really is the Spore King.

I try to run, but the neon chasms in the earth open wider. I zig around a newly formed ravine, heading for the clearing. When the spore fog finally clears, Lydia, Charles, and their men drip with fuzzy white. The first flecks of turquoise flicker around Lydia's lips.

Albert plods toward her and takes her hand. "This way, Dr. Croft. We've got a big order to fill."

The men in the shredded yellow suits follow Albert in step with the other workers. At the end of the row is a glowing boy in bright orange rain boots. It's Nate. Joining the Spore King and leaving me all alone. For good.

Even though I know it's stupid, I jog through the field, dodging the glowing cracks in the earth. When I'm close enough, I half-whisper, half-scream, "Nate, don't!"

His head tilts and he blinks back at me. "Mags?"

Taniesha Jones from the deli counter pivots toward my voice. Her eyelashes are dusted with spores. "Sir. There's another."

Nate's face twists up like he's fighting a massive sneeze. "Run, Mags."

Down the line of workers, heads zing my way. The entire procession shifts and stares at me with cloudy eyes.

CHAPTER THIRTY-THREE

Albert's voice rings through the trees. "I've given you all the time I can spare, Magnolia. You're mine."

I turn and sprint. The ground splits and lime-green mushrooms rise from the cracks. They spread wide like umbrellas opening in a nightmare storm. The center of each has a gaping mouth that pumps out swirling fog.

My lungs burn, and my feet sting where blisters are cropping up on my toes. I come around a bend and spot the crop duster. The Vitaccino van is parked nearby, and the MegaBlaster 3000s lie abandoned on the ground by the driver's-side door. I almost run for them. Until I remember that the fungicide won't do me any good now.

The air stirs, and I spin around, expecting to see Albert and his workers at my heels. Instead, it's the bats. They've come out of the cave and are flapping overhead like a swarm of stirred-up bees.

Voices shout out in the woods behind me. My eyes flick

to the opening of the cave. At least it should be mostly empty. As I slide inside, a trio of workers skulks by.

"Where'd she go?"

I slink back farther. The space reeks like sweaty gym socks, and something wet and gooey mashes under my boots.

"Check the crop duster," one says.

After some more stomping, a pair of sneakers appears in front of the opening. I press myself against the rock, hoping to disappear into the shadows. A heap of bat pellets slides off the cave wall and trickles down my neck. I press my lips together to keep from squealing.

Finally, the sneakers retreat and the voices drift away until all that's left is the bats' squeaks and flaps.

There's a buzzing at my side. I freeze. Earlier, Nate said he felt a buzz in his bones. Just before the fungus sucked him in. The vibration stops and I exhale. Then it's back. I blink into the darkness. There's a faint glow coming from my backpack. I unzip the front pouch. It's Ezra's cell phone. I snatch it up and press the phone to my ear.

"Dad!"

"Magnolia? Where's Ezra?"

"Long story—now's not exactly the best time."

"But on your message you said you were in trouble. That a fungus is spreading through town. That Ezra's sick and that things aren't safe and that you were gonna try to fix it all? I called at Gramma's place and then Nate's. I'm so glad I finally found you." Dad sounds like he's in full-blown panic mode. And for the first time it hits me: Being away is just as hard on him. Dad was always the first one to help us when we needed it. Now he can't do a thing. "Were you really serious about all that?"

I could try to hide the truth from Dad, but he has a right to know what might happen to his family if I can't pull off this rescue. "I was. And it's even worse than I said."

"Worse than a mutant fungus turning your brother into a zombie?" His voice is muffled and there's a woman talking in the background. It sounds like she's telling him to sit down.

"Is everything okay, Dad?"

"Don't worry about me. Fill me in."

I rattle out everything from Old Man Bell's death to Vitaccino's secret ingredient to Albert Eldridge taking over in the woods and the fungicide not working anymore.

"That's a doozy," Dad says. "I always thought something fishy was going on at the plant, but I could never prove it. Of course, that doesn't help you now. What you need is a new remedy."

"Any ideas?"

Dad mutters to himself and I can picture him rubbing his chin with that deep-in-thought look he gets. "When everything happened with the rats, I did some research on fungus. It might not be anything, but I read an article about frogs who survived a fungal infection because of the bacteria on their skin. You might be able to formulate a bacteria-phage serum—"

"I don't even know what that means, Dad. I don't have time to go to a lab or—"

"I'm gonna help you through this, Mags. We need to find something that can kill the fungus. Something that—"

"Sir, I already told you, you can't be on that phone." The woman's back and she sounds ticked.

"But I'm speaking to my daughter and she needs—"

"We have rules for a reason. I'm taking your phone for the duration."

"But ma'am, please—" There's a rustling, then the distant sound of Dad calling out, "Don't give up, Mags!"

The line goes dead.

And just like that, I'm on my own again. Without Nate. Without a plan. Without a glimmer of hope for solving this. I slump against the cave wall. The best I can do is make my way back into town and see if there are any uninfected grown-ups who might be able to help.

I poke my head out of the cave. The bats swoop down like bits of night sky tumbling to the ground. They're about the only thing around here that's not glowing. I glance behind me. Them, and the cave.

In fact, there's no fungi here at all. I creep to the crop

duster, looking at the place where Nate noticed the shriveled mushrooms. I'd figured some fungicide had leaked and killed them. But that stuff quit working. Which means there's gotta be something else killing the mushrooms.

A bat chirps as it dives for a fluttering brown moth. Goose bumps prick along my arms. This is the only place in the woods we've spotted bats.

I reach into my pocket and pull out the crinkled sheets from Dad's journal. If he were here he'd probably know exactly what to do. But since he's not, I've got to try to think like him. On my feet.

The bats just might be the answer. I pace in front of their cave. They haven't grown stalks. They don't glow. But they fly around the woods eating all sorts of bugs that have definitely been exposed to Ophio. Somehow, they're naturally resistant. But how?

My boot squishes into a mound of bat guano. As I fling off the sticky pellets, I think about what Dad said about the frogs who survived a fungal attack because of the bacteria on their skin. I wipe the side of my boot against a rock. Poo's loaded with bacteria.

It would take months of research to be 100 percent sure, but I don't have months. I've got minutes. And a gut-zinging hunch that the microbes in the bat's guano might kill Ophiocordyceps and keep the bats from being infected.

I bend over and scoop up a handful. It rolls around on my glove. This is not the way I imagined my big break-through to go, but science isn't always pretty.

Footsteps tromp through the woods in the distance. It's go out on a limb or turn into a spore-spewing zombie.

I kneel and lift one of the MegaBlasters from the dirt. I bite my lip. Sticky little guano pellets aren't exactly going to squirt out real well. I peek into the Vitaccino van. There's a few water bottles on the floor, plus two coffee thermoses in the cup holders. It'll have to do. I swing the door open and divide the water and coffee between two blasters and head for the cave.

When I finish dropping the pellets into the blasters, I give them a hard shake to stir it all up. It's the best I can do. I've still got a few packs of water grenades, but I'm all out of liquid to mix with them. I move the grenades to the outside pouch and open my bag wide.

"I can't believe I'm doing this." I grab another handful of guano and drop it into my backpack. I keep at it until my bag is completely full of the brown pellets. At least I've got plenty of ammo for a reload.

I hoist the MegaBlasters over both shoulders and march through the woods. The forest is so still I can hear every breath I take. I'm on my own, surrounded by zombi-fied townspeople with a crackpot cure as my only defense. I suck in a breath and force my feet to keep going until

Old Man Bell's cabin peeks out from between the dark branches. I tiptoe closer. A handful of workers lift wooden crates into the backs of two flatbed trucks.

The national order. People all over the country are going to get the new spore-filled recipe. If that shipment goes out, the infection rates will skyrocket. I scan the faces around the trucks. There's no sign of Ezra, Nate, or Albert Eldridge.

The weathervane staked in the yard whirls and something dark shifts in front of the window inside the cabin. A flash of Nate's curly hair.

I wait until the workers' backs are to me, then creep behind some overgrown bushes and make my way to the cabin. The porch creaks as I step on a loose floorboard. Heads swing in my direction. I press against the wood and hold my breath. After a moment, they go back to loading boxes.

The door is partially open and I push it wider with my hip. The air inside smells old and damp like a storm shelter that's been shut up too long. Shadows fall from a faded rocking chair and music drones from an old-fashioned record player. It's a song I've heard Gramma sing, but it sounds different here—like it's coming out at the wrong speed. Too slow and deep.

"Sugar, ah honey honey . . ."

I yank up the arm of the record player and stop the

music. Footprints mark the dusty hall, and there's a soft rustling up ahead. I hold my finger against the Mega-Blasters' triggers and follow the footprints to a closed door. I open it. A staircase leads to blackness. Going down is just plain dumb. Like a fly buzzing directly into a spider's web. I take a step back, but a moan rises from below.

"Maggie." It's Nate. Only different. Flatter, colder. "I've been waiting for you. Come on. I'm stuck. It hurts."

I shouldn't go.

"Please, Mags. Don't leave me here."

I can't stop myself. I feel for the first step, then the next. Nate's cries get louder and my feet move faster. I stumble over the last stair and skid onto a cool concrete floor. It's dark, and there's a dripping sound. "Nate?! Are you here?"

A light flickers and the basement goes from inky black to fluorescent green. "We're all here now," Albert croons. "One big, happy family. At last."

CHAPTER THIRTY-FOUR

Twisting ribbons of fungi wind across the basement walls like nuclear centipedes. Nate slumps on the concrete behind Albert. His shoulders sag and his mouth droops, making him look like somebody's tossed-out ragdoll. Ezra stands at Albert's side, his eyes glassy.

I point one blaster at Albert. "Let them go!"

"I can't do that. They mean too much to me."

Nate's eyes shift to mine. "Run," he mouths.

I put my finger on the MegaBlaster's trigger, ready to soak them all. But something falls from above. Cold scales scrape against my neck as a foot-long black snake coils down my chest. I scream, reaching for its tail with both hands. The blasters crash to the ground and Ezra kicks them away. I fling the snake toward the corner of the basement.

"It's only a little reptile. Nothing to fear."

I scramble up a few steps as a puff of alligator-green dust swirls around Albert's ankles. I press my bandanna close to my nose. Albert opens his mouth and the first curl of wispy white tumbles out. I hurtle up two more steps, but the spore cloud whirls up fast after me.

"Stop!" Nate cries from below. He's on his feet and gripping one of the blasters. "Leave Maggie alone!"

"Maggie?" Ezra presses his hand against the side of his head like he's waking up with a whopping migraine.

"It's too late for doubts," Albert says. "We're all in this together. Get the weapon from the boy, Ezra."

Ezra jerks his head from me to Nate, then trudges over. But before he can grab the MegaBlaster, Nate pulls the trigger. There's a whizzing sound and then . . . *splat*. Brown liquid splashes Ezra's face and he stumbles back.

Nate squirts him again and the mixture fizzes and bubbles as it sinks into Ezra's skin. The Day-Glo blue fades from his lips and he blinks at me, looking more like himself than he has in days.

"What's that stink?" Nate asks, sniffing the end of the blaster.

"Bat guano." I stand and meet Albert's murky eyes. "You're not the only one with a new recipe."

"Get away from my friend." Nate points the squirt gun at Albert.

Albert gives a moldy smile. "It's been a pleasure, but I must be going now." There's a rush of wind. I squeeze my eyes shut and when I open them again a cloud of white vapor hangs in the air. Albert's gone.

Ezra sits up and rubs one eye. "Maggie? What's going on?"

"No time to explain." I trot down the stairs, grab the other blaster, and turn to Nate, who still gleams cerulean. "Close your eyes. It's about to get real stinky."

"What do you mean it's—"

I pull the trigger and drench him in guano. It sizzles and foams over Nate's entire body.

"That stings, Mags!" He wriggles around like I've just dropped a pile of fire ants down his shorts.

"You'll thank me later." I keep spraying until his arms and legs are coated in a goopy layer of liquid brown. When I finally quit, he slumps to the floor with a groan. "I smell like my Uncle Tony's house after his sewer system got clogged."

I can't argue with that, but it worked. At least, I think it worked. Neither of them glows anymore and the guano hasn't burned through their skin or turned them into jerky. "How do you feel?"

Nate scratches the back of his head. "I'd kill for a bag of pizza rolls and a two-liter of root beer right now."

I smile. "If we get outta here, I'll buy you all the pizza rolls you can snarf." There's a rattling outside the cabin. The fungi on the basement walls fan out and creep down the floor toward us. If I had more ammo, I'd spray it all down too. "We gotta move."

We trot up the stairs and into the living room. The record's spinning again, only now it's crazy fast and high-pitched.

I grab the record and snap it over my knee.

The porch creaks. I pull back the curtains and peek out. Taniesha and Kirby plod back and forth in front of the door like a couple of sleepwalking soldiers. "We need to start spraying the rest of them."

Ezra glances from the blaster in my hand to the one in Nate's. "I can't fight empty-handed."

I swing my backpack to the ground and pull out the packs of water grenades. "The rest of the bag's loaded with ammo. Just mix with water. Should be enough to treat all the workers."

"On it." Ezra grabs the bag from me, then pauses. "Mags?"

"Yeah?"

His eyes are soft and hopeful like the Ezra I remember from before Dad left. "I'm sorry . . . about, well, you know."

I nod. "You're forgiven." I grab the doorknob and pause. "Mostly."

I push the door open. Taniesha and Kirby stalk toward us, and I soak them with the MegaBlaster. They sizzle and squeal. A red-haired boy a couple of years older than Ezra leaps onto the porch and Nate fires a steady brown stream in his face. As the guano drips down his chin, he blinks back at us. "Where am I?"

"In the middle of a battle." I hop down the steps,

charging toward the flatbed trucks. We can't let them make that delivery.

Nate's singing under his breath. "When there's something weird in ol' Shady Pines. Who you gonna call? Spore Busters!"

I shake my head. "It's good to have you back."

Jack and Zion are still loading crates into the back of the truck. We spray them, and they try to scutter away but we keep at it until they're coated in drippy brown. I go to squirt some sludgy guano on the tires, but my blaster runs dry. "How much ammo do you have left?" I call.

Nate tugs on his trigger a few times. Nothing comes out. "About that much."

The red-haired boy we just drenched trots our way. "Anything I can do to help?"

Nate and I exchange a glance. "How do you feel about bat poop?"

"Better than I do about fungus."

Jack and Zion sit up. Jack wipes a blob of guano-coffee mix from his eyebrow. "We wanna help too."

I tell them where to find more guano and they grab the buckets they used for picking mushrooms and jog out into the forest.

Ezra trots down the porch carrying the over-stuffed backpack. "You guys ready for a reload?"

"Perfect timing." Nate and I scoop out a few grenades.

Ezra nods toward the back of the truck. "I'm gonna dump these cases of Vitaccino. Make sure they never get out."

"Not so fast. That's private property." Lydia Croft steps out from behind one of the trucks. A star-shaped fungus pulses at her temple.

"Ah, man," Nate says. "Looks like we have a Spore Queen in the works."

"Not today, we don't." I fling two squishy grenades and pelt Lydia in the face.

She sizzles like the rest. "What's the meaning of this? How dare you!" A dollop of brown goo drips from her nose. I hurl another grenade for good measure. She sinks to the ground, looking around at the dumped-out boxes and puddles of spilled Vitaccino. "All my work. Ruined."

"You shoulda thought of that before you loaded your health drinks with mutant fungus," Nate says, then launches a pair of grenades my way.

I spin around and catch Charles Croft creeping up behind me. Nate's grenades pelt him, and Charles hollers and smacks at his skin. "Vitaccino's been around longer than you've been alive. This is far from over."

The wind howls and electric teal races up the trunk of every tree.

"I couldn't agree more." Albert Eldridge slinks out from the shadows.

CHAPTER THIRTY-FIVE

Albert is completely covered in mossy white, except for two glittering emerald eyes. Thorny spikes sprout all over his body. Like a fungus porcupine. As he walks, the spikes fling off him.

"Don't come any closer." I lift a grenade.

A laugh bellows through the forest and Albert rises up like mist drifting just above the ground. The grenades burst on the dirt. "Fungus has one job in this world. Decomposing. Rotting. Devouring. Until nothing remains but it."

"And that's why nobody likes you." Nate fires another grenade. This one zings Albert in the shoulder, knocking off a few white spikes and sending them flying.

The earth cracks and a fleshy blue fungus with octopus-like tentacles spurts from the crevasse. "Do you know what the largest living organism in the world is?"

Nate reaches for another grenade. "Why do I get the feeling he's gonna say it's a fungus?"

More dirt falls away from the crevasse, making the

break at least three feet wide. It ripples with fluorescent light, and murky fog rises up. "What you see with your eye is only the tip of the iceberg. The rest lies deep in the earth. Waiting for the opportune moment to blossom again."

"Well, that's not gonna happen." I shake the bag, pouring out more grenades. I look from Nate to Ezra. "On the count of three."

The spore cloud plumes higher until the whole forest looks like a smoking volcano.

"One, two—"

Albert opens his mouth.

"Three!"

Our grenades soar through the air. The first hits Albert's leg. It sizzles, but the cyclone of white keeps coming. The next hits his neck, then one to the cheek. His skin bubbles like a science experiment gone wrong. I hurl another. It soars directly into his gaping mouth. Brown explodes around his milky face. He staggers to his knees.

Another flurry of grenades zooms his way, and Albert howls. The trees join in, making the whole forest shriek so loudly I drop the grenade I'm holding and slap my hands over my ears.

Albert crawls toward the wide crack in the earth like a cockroach retreating from a can of Raid. "You could have been an ambassador between my world and yours,

Magnolia Stone. The harbinger of a new species." Albert's white spiky stalks fizzle, then fall away. He stretches out a misty hand that's nearly transparent.

"It's like he's nothing but spores," Nate says.

Albert's eyes flick from blazing green to pale blue to brown. "Say hello to your father for me. . . . He was a good man." His words sound like moaning wind. There's a sizzle and then the shape of Albert Eldridge puffs away entirely. A rain cloud chased back by the sun. The forest's shimmering lights sputter then go dark. We stand in silence for several long, heavy minutes.

"Is he gone?" Ezra asks.

"I don't know." I creep toward the break in the ground. Only the dark flesh of the mushrooms remains. They shiver then wilt in on themselves until it's dry, crusted ground.

We slump to the dirt.

We did it.

We stopped the Spore King. I didn't lose Nate or Ezra. Somehow, we all made it through.

"What about the rest of the town?" Nate asks. "We're going to need a lot more bat poop to clean up Shady Pines."

I nod and scan the crowd of newly cured workers. They hang around the field, blinking at one another. Kirby from the fire department leans against a tree, looking like he's just woken up from a hundred-year sleep. I chew my lip. A guy with access to dozens of feet of hose and lots of big trucks could come in pretty handy about now. "We need to put them to work."

"What do you have in mind?" Nate asks, and I notice he's pulled out his camcorder and is panning over the crowd. He catches my eye and grins. "Never miss an opportunity for a great shot."

The old Nate is back for sure.

I cut across the field to Kirby. "How you feeling?"

He rubs his head. "Been better."

"I might know a way we can kill the rest of the fungi, but I'm gonna need some help."

"Just name it."

Moonlight spills over us as we arrive in the clearing. I turn to Nate and Ezra. "You think you can handle one more stop?"

Ezra reaches for his skateboard. "I'm pretty sure I owe you one."

Nate and I exchange a knowing look as we hop on our bikes.

The Wormery's windows are still coated in a film of white. I untie the knotted shoelaces holding the doors closed and pull the last two grenades from my bag. Nate and Ezra raise their blasters as we push through the doors. Bubba Bass flips his tail and starts to sing.

"Mac?" I call.

"You sure this is safe?" Ezra eyes the faintly glowing walls and knocked-over fishing poles.

"Not really." The door separating the back room from the register creaks, and my heart hiccups.

"Can I help y'all?" Mac emerges from the workroom, his powdery stalk bobbing as he walks.

"Yikes!" Ezra jumps back.

I launch the grenades at Mac. "This might sting a bit."

We coat Mac in goo and he hollers while dancing a wild jig. After a moment, he blinks as if seeing us for the first time. He rubs one hand over the back of his neck. The stalk crumbles and falls to the ground. "Magnolia? Is that you?"

"Hi, Mac." I smile. "It's good to see you again."

Mac tilts his head, taking in his fungi-filled shop. "I got a feeling there's a story that goes along with all this."

I reach for my backpack and dump a load of guano pellets on the counter. "This'll help with the cleanup. Kirby from the fire department can get you more soon."

Mac lets out a low whistle. "You kids really are something else."

When we reach our trailers, Gramma's on the porch, cell phone in one hand and a butcher knife in the other. She squints at us, then drops the knife and races to me. She wraps me up in her arms and squeezes so tight I cough.

"I've been calling the sheriff and that Croft woman and anyone else in town I could think of. Nobody's picking up."

The first pink rays of dawn break over the trailer park. "It's been a long night, Gramma."

She sniffs. "What's that smell?" She pulls back and runs her eyes from me to Nate to Ezra. My trash bag suit is ripped and I can feel all sorts of twigs and leaves in my hair. All three of us drip with liquid guano.

"Remember that fungus I was talking about? Well—"

"On second thought." She runs a shaky hand over her mess of silver hair. "I think this is a tale that can wait till later. Showers. Hot ones. Then to bed with you all."

Nate's front door flings open and his dad sticks out his head. "Any news, Trudi?"

"They're back!" Gramma calls. "They smell terrible, but they're okay."

Nate wriggles free from Gramma. "I think I'd better head back to my place. Dad's probably got a couple of questions."

We trot up the porch steps and open the front door. Pacing the floor is a scruffy-faced man in a park ranger's shirt and khakis. When he spots me, he turns and closes the distance between us.

"Dad!" I stretch to my tippy toes, wrap my arms around

his shoulders, and hold on tight like I'm freefalling and he's my one parachute. "You came!"

"The taxi just dropped me off and I was about to run out the door looking for you all." His cheeks are rough with stubble, and he smells like pine needles and shaving cream. For a moment, everything that happened in the forest fades away. "Sorry we got cut off earlier. Those flight attendants mean business."

"You were right about the bacteria killing Ophio and the rats and Vitaccino and the Crofts. And Albert Eldridge . . . he wasn't a man anymore, he was—" My voice breaks and a shudder runs down my back.

"It's all right. I'm here now." Dad hugs me tight. "Everything's going to be okay."

I press my face into the solidness of his chest, and tears I didn't know were there start to stream down. When I finally pull back, my eyes feel puffy and my nose drips.

Gramma puts a light hand on my shoulder. Her eyes glisten. "I'm glad you children are all right. Now I need some time to talk to your daddy. Showers and bed. Tomorrow's a new day. There'll be plenty of time for telling stories then."

Dad presses his lips to the top of my head. "I'm proud of you, Magnolia." He looks to Ezra. "Both of you."

Ezra dips his head and peers down at his feet. "It's good to see you, Dad."

"You too, Ezra." I step back as Dad opens his arms. Ezra pauses for a second then takes the three steps to him. Dad pulls Ezra close and wraps him in a bear hug.

I smile and push a sticky bit of hair off my forehead. Things are going to be different. I don't know how exactly. But the Spore King is gone, and Dad's here. That's gotta be worth something.

I head for the bathroom, but halfway down the hall, Ezra grabs my arm. "Wait up."

"If you're planning to call dibs on the first shower, you've got another think coming," I say with a half grin.

"Shower's all yours. I just wanted to say . . . thanks." Ezra rubs the back of his hair. "I wouldn't have made it out of there if you hadn't come for me."

"You're worth it, I guess." I smile and reach for the door handle. "But don't go getting a big head about it."

"A big head's better than a spore head."

I shudder. "Never say those words again, please."

He gives my arm a little shove and grins. "I think I can manage that."

EPILOGUE

Ezra's getting stronger, but there's still something a little different about him. Sometimes I catch him staring across the room with a daydreaming look in his eye. I think the forest took a piece of him, or maybe being part fungus for a while just sorta changes a person.

Dad had to fly back to Wyoming after a week, but he says we're all going to live under one roof again soon. Before he left, he designed a contraption to help the fire department spray the guano mix around town and get rid of the rest of the fungus.

But his visit wasn't all work. We also kayaked at Lake Williams, watched sci-fi movies, and ate junk food. Dad and Ezra even made a campfire and grilled hot dogs for everybody. We talked a lot too. Sometimes about science and sometimes about the things that science can't really explain.

After the outbreak, Vitaccino was closed down for

good. The news stations ran tons of stories about the Crofts, who had a few other shady operations going on besides breeding mutant fungus. And who are sitting in jail now, as is the rest of the board.

Gramma never did want to hear all the details about what happened that night. But lately, she's cooking more than ever. Oodles of casseroles and unending puddings and pies. This morning alone she fixed pancakes, French toast, biscuits and gravy, bacon, and fruit parfaits.

As Gramma piles another stack of bacon on Ezra's plate, the doorbell rings. I swallow a bite of strawberry. "I'll get it."

I push open the screen door and Nate waves. "Hey, Mags. You got a minute?"

"Always." I step out onto the porch, and we sit on the bottom step together. Our legs stretch toward the weedy lawn. "How's it going?"

He folds his arms behind his neck, looking supremely satisfied. "My latest video just hit ten thousand views."

"The one about vampire robots from outer space?"

"That's the one." Nate grins. "I've made twenty bucks off ads already."

"That's awesome!"

"Yeah." His eyes drift to the clubhouse and he sighs. We scrubbed it down with the bat guano solution, then soaked it in bleach. Even so, neither of us have spent much time in it since the outbreak. "You think you and Ezra might really move to Yellowstone?"

"I don't know. Maybe."

I'm not sure what the future holds. But right now, the sun's shining, everyone's healthy, and there's still a month of summer vacation. That's enough for me.

Nate's quiet a moment, then he turns to me with a sideways smile. "So, I was talking to Ricky this morning over Eggos. He saw something weird last night at the old roller skating rink."

I chew my thumbnail, then glance out over the trailer park. Glory, Nate's basset hound, snores on his porch. Splashes and squeals rise from the Marble Falls pool in the distance. I lean back against the step. "Tell me everything."

AUTHOR'S NOTE

Like Maggie, I grew up with a scientist dad who often discussed bits of research or new discoveries around the dinner table. I didn't follow in his footsteps and go to medical school or get a degree in biochemistry, but I did develop an interest in scientific happenings, particularly of the weird or unexplained variety.

While *The Mutant Mushroom Takeover* is fictional, a number of the details are based on real science.

For starters, *Ophiocordyceps unilateralis* is an actual fungus that was first discovered almost two hundred years ago infecting ants in tropical forests. As in the book, the fungus causes a stroma stalk to grow from its victim's head. The fungus then takes over the ant's brain, persuading it to bite down on a leaf near its colony. The stalk then ruptures, raining down infectious spores.

While in real life Ophiocordyceps doesn't glow, there are more than eighty species of **bioluminescent fungi** that can be found in forests all around the world. The chemical that causes the glow, oxyluciferin, is the same stuff found in fireflies and glowing underwater creatures. The mushrooms don't just shimmer for kicks; the light also helps the fungus lure in bugs, which spread the spores to new locations. That sounds like a tactic Albert Eldridge would approve of.

Toward the end of the book, Albert alludes to another true-to-life detail—the world's largest living organism, *Armillaria ostoyae*, also known as the **Humongous Fungus**. It's located in Oregon's Malheur National Forest, stretches 2,385 acres (nearly four miles), and weighs 35,000 tons. That's as much as nearly 3,000 of the world's heaviest elephants.

During their investigation, Maggie and Nate discover two curiously named species, **dog vomit slime mold** and **stinkhorn mushrooms**, both of which are real. I've encountered each of them in my own yard in Texas, and believe me, they deserve their names.

It's also true that trees communicate with one another using a **vast fungal network**. While they don't take down signs or fashion handcuffs out of their roots, they do occasionally sabotage enemy plants by releasing toxins into the earth. But generally, the fungi-tree relationship is mutually beneficial for all. The trees get better access to water and nutrient-rich soil while the fungi get to feed from the trees' roots.

Hive mind is also real and exists in insects like bees and ants. Using their collective intelligence, the entire colony functions as a single entity, making the most of their resources and defenses, not unlike the zombified hosts in *The Mutant Mushroom Takeover*.

And finally, **bacteria really can knock out some nasty**

fungal infections. For example, many bats infected with white-nose syndrome, a fungal disease that's killed millions of North American bats, have been saved by a remedy made from the bacterium *Pseudomonas fluorescens*. Likewise, researchers discovered that Panamanian frogs infected with a potent fungus could be healed using the bacteria found on their own skin.

ACKNOWLEDGMENTS

This book was such fun to write and I'm grateful to all those who played a part in helping it come to life, whether it was listening to random fungi facts, reading an early draft, or just being excited that I was writing a novel.

For my wise and hard-working agent, Alyssa Eisner Henkin, thank you for your enthusiasm for this story and for seeing all the ways it could be even stronger. I'm so grateful to have you by my side. To Alice Fugate, for all your attention to detail and assistance.

To my editor, Krista Vitola, thank you for making this book a reality. This manuscript has greatly benefited from your expertise, care, and excitement. I'm delighted to be working with you. To the Simon & Schuster BFYR team, including Catherine Laudine, Kendra Levin, Beth Adelman, and Katrina Groover, thank you for your hard work and valuable insights.

For my sweet husband, thank you for always believing in me. You give me courage to believe too. I love you. For my children who view life with humor and wonder. You inspire me to write and to hope for good things for the world.

To my mom whose gift of storytelling filled my childhood with quirky characters and the sights and sounds of other places and times. To my dad, for inspiring an interest in science and for kindly brainstorming with me about icky things like bacteriophages and parasites. To my creative, talented, and super-cool brother, who was my earliest hero. To Glenn and Jolene, thank you for always being interested in what I'm up to and believing in me. For Carrie, Natalie, Brad, JT, and Sihyun, thank you for your encouragement along the way. To Lauren Anderson, for all the book chats and for being a true kindred spirit.

Thank you to my amazing critique partners and earliest readers, Liz Edelbrock, Lauren LeBlanc, Helen Jameson, and Andrea Rand. Go Dots and Dashes, go!

To the Pitch Wars community, for its continual boosting up of writers and most especially to Kim Long and Jennifer Brown, for being some of Maggie's first and most enthusiastic supporters. Thank you for all the shared mushroom GIFs, squeals over good news, and words of wisdom. And to Shelly Steig, K. C. Held, April Clausen, Jessica Olson, Megan Clements, Lorelei Savaryn, and Mindy Thompson for being cheerleaders and sounding boards along the way.

For my fellow writers, Kayla Olson, Taylor Morris, Amber Wessling, Eric Boyd, Christina Dwivedi, Marjorie Stordeur, and Heather Kelley, thank you for your advice and encouragement.

And finally, to the One who is my light in the darkness and peace in the storm, you are the giver of every good and perfect gift.

Turn the page for a sneak peek at
Attack of the Killer Komodos.

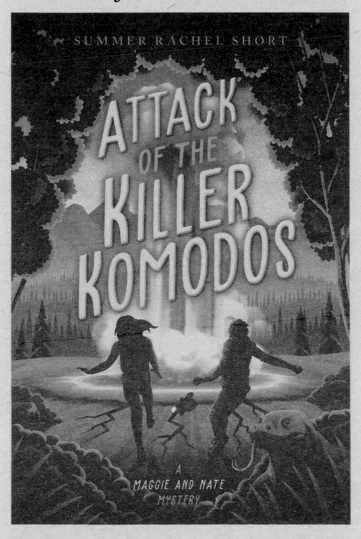

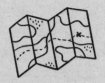

Water the color of bullfrogs gurgles against my shins as we slog across the Firehole River. Nate swings a rope in an unruly figure eight and bellows a Bigfoot call that sounds like a dying whoopee cushion sputtering out its final serenade.

I zoom in the video camera as he takes a wobbly step toward the riverbank. The smell of pine sap and spicy sagebrush mingles with my SPF 75 and citronella bug spray.

We've been in Yellowstone National Park less than twenty-four hours, and we're already on the hunt for the legendary primate. As an up-and-coming naturalist, I'm skeptical about the big guy's existence, but humoring Nate is number three on my Yellowstone Vacation Bucket List. Plus, hanging out in the wilds of the park is basically my definition of paradise.

"You getting all this, Mags?" Nate calls over his shoulder. He's got on dark shades and a few streaks of black paint spread across his freckled cheeks, plus a neon green

I BELIEVE T-shirt that pretty much cancels out the camo face paint. "Make sure you get a close-up of the mini grappling hook."

"Already on it, partner," I say, giving him a thumbs up. I've recently signed on as the production manager for Nate's YouTube channel, *The Conspiracy Squad*. The pay is squat, and the working conditions are questionable. But investigating the unexplained is kinda our thing, though Nate's tastes run more to the otherworldly than mine. The show's dedicated to freaky, weird, and potentially made-up happenings. It used to be small potatoes, but ever since a mutated zombie fungus spread through our hometown six weeks ago, *The Conspiracy Squad* has been getting more attention. Nate's even had a couple of companies reach out to him looking to sponsor segments, hence the rope and grappling hook. My latest contribution to the show is a segment I've dubbed "Maggie's Minute." At the end of each episode, I give a few tidbits that offer a scientific explanation for whatever paranormal finding Nate's reporting on. He even made me some cool intro music. Fans seem to dig it. Though I do get a lot of questions about the Bermuda Triangle and the Lost City of Atlantis. I haven't come up with good explanations for those just yet. But the world's full of mysteries. Like sand dunes that make songs that sound like chanting monks or the way birds can find their way home after traveling thousands of miles without ever using a map or GPS.

I record another minute of Nate stomping around and belching out grunts that sound more like indigestion than primate calls. I glance up from the camcorder. "You might wanna go easy on the sound effects if you really want a shot at attracting an elusive species."

"Lots of Squatchers have tried that route and got diddly to show for it. My strategy is to go in loud and proud. Let the hairy dude know I mean business." Nate whirls in a dramatic spin, his rope high, like an eleven-year-old mythical beast wrangler.

As I wipe a spray of river water from the camera's screen, my stomach rumbles and I think about Dad back at the campsite grilling up lunch. This week's going to be our first chance in a long while to really kick back and spend some time together. He's promised me a hike this afternoon and marshmallow roasting over the campfire after that—numbers one and two on the bucket list.

Nate suddenly stops gyrating and points to a scattering of evergreens along the riverbank. "Mags," he hisses. "I think there might really be something out here."

"It's probably just a squirrel or a muskrat," I say, but narrow my eyes and scan the tree line anyway. Lately, disaster has a way of sniffing us out quicker than a gang of mosquitoes on a sticky summer's night.

Nate edges to the shore. "If my gut's singing the tune

I think it is, this just might be our big breakthrough."

Nate's gut is notoriously unpredictable. Especially after half a bag of Flamin' Hot Cheezy Poppers. The sagebrush rustles, and a cloud of dust puffs out. My heart hiccups. I'm not expecting Bigfoot, but Yellowstone's got a few real-deal hazards. Before we piled into Gramma's Ford for the fifteen-hundred-mile trip out to visit Dad, I did loads of research. Thermal pools brimming with scalding hot water. Territorial moose and grumpy bison. Packs of roaming wolves. And the head honcho of the Yellowstone predators, the grizzly.

"Careful, Nate. We don't want a run-in with a mama bear."

Nate ignores me and tiptoes closer. "All the urban legends say Bigfoot hangs out near food and water. We've got the river, and there's a load of half-munched berries on the ground." He pauses and sniffs. "Yeti B.O."

I skid up to the shore, water slopping out the sides of my sneakers. "Don't go stirring anything up until I get there!"

"This dude reeks!" Nate pokes his toe into a clump of prickly brush.

I sniff. "I don't think that's a Bigfoot. That smells like—"

"Skunk!" Nate scrambles back as a black-and-white tail emerges from the sage.

A skunk is better than a grizzly, but not by much. I

shove the video camera into my backpack and thrust my nose into my T-shirt. "Gramma's gonna kill me if we come back to the campground stinking like skunk rump."

The tail scoots forward, but no fluffy rodent body follows. Instead, a hulking reptile emerges, skunk tail clasped between its scaly jaws. The lizard swoops toward Nate with a clumsy, swishing trot.

"Get back!" I snatch a branch off the ground. The lizard spits out the skunk's severed tail but keeps charging our way. A long, yellow tongue with a distinct fork swishes out of its mouth.

"You never told me Yellowstone had baby Godzillas!" Nate backpedals from the beady-eyed giant.

The lizard's as long as an alligator and has to weigh a few hundred pounds. Stringy saliva drips from its jowls. This thing shouldn't be here. The Yellowstone guidebook I read on the way up said the park only had one species of lizard. A tiny, bug-eating critter that could fit in the palm of my hand.

This thing is in a whole other league.

Massive. Foul drool. Definitely carnivorous. I wrack my brain trying to remember all the research I did about lizards back when I bought my pet leopard gecko. Only one lizard fits the bill, and it's native to Indonesia. "It's a Komodo dragon," I breathe.

Nate's eyes go wide, and I can practically hear the conspiracy theories bubbling around in his skull. "Did you just confirm the existence of dragons? Because if you did—" Nate stumbles over the rope's grappling hook and crashes to the ground, his flip-flop soaring into the air.

I thrust my arm out to Nate. "They don't breathe fire or fly. But they're fast and have huge appetites."

The Komodo dragon whips forward and sinks its slimy teeth into Nate's sandal.

Nate grips my arm and leaps to his feet. We bolt, abandoning the rope and Nate's flip-flop.

"How'd that thing get here?" Nate pants as we turn around and slosh back through the river. "Somebody's pet get loose?"

"Nobody in their right mind would keep a Komodo dragon as a pet. Their bites are loaded with venom that causes their victims to die a slow, gruesome death."

Nate peers back at where we left the hulking reptile. "Maybe we could save the nature lesson for later, Mags."

I follow his gaze. A long, dark form swishes into the river after us.

"There's one more thing," I call as we break into a watery sprint. "Komodo dragons are fantastic swimmers."

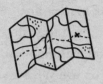

The dragon disappears under the swirling green water. We scramble through the river faster and are nearly to the opposite shore when Nate shrieks and crumples down with a splash. He stretches out one arm. "Run, Mags! It's chomping me up whole!"

I drop to my hands and knees. Cold water spills over my shorts. I scoop up a rock and scan the river, ready to pelt the scaly fiend if I have to. But instead of razor sharp teeth piercing Nate's leg, there's a tangle of weeds wrapped around his ankle in a slippery, green knot. I drop the rock and tear away the plants. "You're okay," I say, my pulse sliding back down to nearly normal.

"False alarm." Nate gives a sheepish smile.

Just then the river erupts as the Komodo dragon thrashes up.

"Ahhhhh!" We scream and spring to our feet.

Water flies off the lizard as it jerks its head from side to side, a rainbow trout wriggling in its jaws.

We go into full-blown cheetah mode, not stopping until we reach the shore. My gaze dashes back to the dragon. It still lingers in the middle of the river. Its black eyes have a feisty look in them that reminds me of my pet gecko when he's munching live crickets.

It flicks out its tongue like it's a connoisseur of fine prey and we're the next course. "Most reptiles only attack when they're hungry or scared. But this one sinks its teeth into everything that strolls its way," I pant.

"This is just like issue 414 of *Midnight Kingdom*, where Brigadier Ajax fought a mechanical piranha warlord. The dude ate Ajax's entire army in a single night. It was brutal." Nate eyes the dragon like a wizened general who's seen one too many battles.

At last, the Komodo swallows down the fish and swishes toward the far riverbank. As it crawls onto land, its back legs emerge from the water. The sun glints off something metallic wrapped around one ankle. I nudge Nate. "Check it out. It's got a tag."

Nate squints. "What does that mean? That the dragon really is a pet?"

"It looks more like the kind of thing scientists use to track wildlife."

"Well, whoever is supposed to be keeping tabs on Captain BiteyPants is majorly blowing it."

I can't argue with that. On top of the lizard being

supersized and extra cranky, it's also a long way from home. As the massive lizard crawls back to the sagebrush, it lowers its neck and picks up something black and white. I squint. It's the grody skunk tail. Clumps of fur fly from the Komodo's mouth as it gulps down the skunk remains.

"Seriously?" Nate shakes his head. "Does that thing ever quit pounding down grub?"

"Let's hope so. The last thing the park needs is an invasive predator shaking things up. We'll fill Dad in as soon as we get back to the campground. He'll know what to do."

Up until six months ago, Dad lived with us in Shady Pines, Texas, but after a big mix-up at his old job, he got fired. He couldn't find a local job and ended up moving out to Yellowstone to work as a park ranger. Having Dad live a thousand miles away is pretty much the worst, but I've already tried fixing things on my own, and that ended up being a huge disaster. So for now I'm trying to be patient and hope things will work themselves out.

Nate arches a brow. "You sure we can trust your dad with this kinda news?"

I roll my eyes. "Not this again." Before we left for Yellowstone, Nate watched some far-fetched documentary claiming there's a conspiracy among park rangers to keep Bigfoot and other urban legends a secret. Now he's convinced Dad's got the inside scoop on Sasquatch. "Dad isn't involved with any conspiracy, and he definitely isn't hiding Bigfoot."

Nate grunts. "According to the documentary, it's always the people you least suspect."

I sigh. Trying to convince Nate to see things from a scientific point of view is a losing battle. "Let's just get to my dad."

Nate frowns. "Once we tell him, that'll be the end of it. My one shot at being a real-deal dragon hunter gone just like that."

"Not a real dragon, remember?"

"Fine, but if that dragon—not to be confused with the mythical, treasure-stealing kind—isn't local, and it isn't somebody's pet, how'd it get here?" Nate asks.

I grip my T-shirt and wring out river water. I've been asking myself the same question. "I don't know. But however it happened, it's not good."

On our way back to the campsite, the forest's dark canopy casts long shadows over us. I sneak a glance over my shoulder, just to be sure nothing scaly is lurking behind us.

Nate lifts his ball cap and runs a hand through his heap of curls. "You didn't happen to catch any of that on camera, did you?"

"I was kinda trying to avoid having my appendages devoured."

"Understandable," Nate says, flopping through the

woods with one bare foot. "Maybe we could re-create the moment back home with your gecko and some super zoomed-in shots. . . ."

Nate's voice drifts off, and he gets a faraway look in his eye, like he's dreaming up an epic scheme. I flash back to a million different adventures we've had over the years. Building the world's greatest treehouse, aka Headquarters, using nothing but scrap wood and discarded odds and ends. Biking the backroads of Shady Pines in search of crop circles. And most recently, saving my brother and the rest of the town from a deadly mutant fungus. Nate and I may not always see things the same way, but somehow we bring out the best in each other anyhow.

Our campsite comes into view—extra-large family tent, a circle of chairs around the campfire, and a bag of food hanging on a pole eight feet high to keep the bears away. Daisy, the yellow mare Dad uses to get around the back county, swishes her tail and gives a low whinny. Before we make it to the tent, I spot my thirteen-year-old brother, Ezra, standing too close to a tree, eyes locked on something small and dark.

"Everything all right?" I ask as the dark thing twitches.

"Not unless you call being injured and majorly out-numbered all right," Ezra answers, and stretches out one hand toward the tree.

I take a closer look. A two-inch cockroach is surrounded by a squad of army ants. I bite my lip. Ever since the fungus invasion, Ezra's been on a mission to save every creepy crawly creature he comes across. That is, when he's not zoned out, staring into space. The cockroach limps and makes a disturbing buzzing sound. "Maybe you should just let nature take its course. Just this once."

Ezra turns to face me, his dark eyes wide. "What if you'd just let nature take its course with me?"

"That was different. You're not a cockroach."

Ezra shakes his head. "I'm helping this guy. End of story."

Nate peeks at the roach and makes a gagging face.

I take a step back. "Have you seen Dad lately? I need to talk to him."

The cockroach creeps onto Ezra's open palm. "Check the tent."

I head that way and am about to unzip the canvas door when I hear hushed voices coming from inside.

"That sounds like a whole mess of trouble, Tommy. You remember what happened back in Shady Pines. You don't want to end up fired again," I hear Gramma say.

"Don't worry, Mom. I've got it all under control. I'm not gonna lose my job," Dad answers.

"From my experience, people always think they've got things under control until they're wrapped up in some big, nasty disaster. If you want my advice, let the thing be somebody else's problem. You've got the kids to think of," Gramma replies. "Somebody could get hurt, and that somebody just might be you."

Dad sighs. "You worry too much."

Before I can decide whether to keep eavesdropping or yank down the zipper and get to the bottom of whatever Gramma and Dad are talking about, there's rustling and the sound of footsteps coming my way. I scramble from the tent and race back to Ezra and Nate. Sweat pricks along my forehead and my head swims. Dad is supposed to be spending quality time with me and Ezra this week, not getting himself tangled up in dangerous shenanigans.

"That was fast," Nate says, looking gloomy. "I guess your dad's gonna zip outta here and capture the thing all Indiana Jones–like."

"I didn't actually tell him about the Komodo yet." I glance over my shoulder, wondering what Dad could possibly be up to that might risk his job.

Nate grins. "You won't regret this. We're gonna get the most killer video ever."

Before I can answer Nate, the tent flap opens. Dad looks around the campsite, spots us, and waves. A twirl of smoke drifts over the camp chairs. Dad makes a sudden beeline for the fire. He grabs a skewer and pokes a blackened hunk. Ash tumbles out of the flames, streaking Dad's gray park ranger shirt and avocado-green pants with soot.

He shakes his head and calls, "These hot dogs aren't looking so good. How do you kiddos feel about ramen and Vienna sausages?"

"Over my dead body." Gramma saunters out of the tent. She's wearing a fuchsia tracksuit and a hefty polka-dot fanny pack. It's what Gramma calls an "outdoorsy" look, but with her silvery hair sprayed into spikes and ginormous gold hoop earrings, she looks ready to walk the Thurston County Outlet Mall, not spend a week in a national park.

Gramma smirks when she catches sight of me and Nate. "You two been mud wrestling some wild boars?"

Nate shoots me a sideways glance. "Just snagging footage for *The Conspiracy Squad*, ma'am."

"Probably tricky to get good video out this way. From what I hear, UFOs hate paying the park entrance fees." Dad chuckles.

Nate tips his ball cap. "Not too shabby, Mr. Stone. I, for one, appreciate a solid dad joke from time to time."

I try to add a little laugh, but only part of me is listening. I need to know the scoop on what's up with Dad.